daisy drama club

SPOTLIGHT!

written and illustrated by
belinda roberts

BEETLEHEART
PUBLISHING
www.beetleheart.co.uk

BEETLEHEART PUBLISHING

Daisy Drama Club - Spotlight!
was first published
in the United Kingdom in 2013
by Beetleheart Publishing.

Whilst this work is inspired by the original Daisy Drama Club
all characters appearing in this work are fictitious.
Any resemblance to real persons, living or dead, is purely coincidental.

ISBN
0-9540208-7-1
978-0-9540208-7-3

Daisy Drama Club - Spotlight! © 2013 Belinda Roberts
The moral right of the author has been asserted.

Illustrations © 2013 Belinda Roberts

www.beetleheart.co.uk

Contents

To all the members
of the original

daisy drama club

Howls in the Wood

The wolf slipped silently between the trees of the dark wood. A ravenous hunger made it tense and alert. It's glittering green eyes narrowed to a slit as it searched out movement of prey between the trees. A flash of red moving nearby caught its attention. Food! The wolf let out a great howl and bounded forward, its sharp teeth bared ready to sink into its victim. The creature in red started and turned to run. Faster and faster through the trees they chased, the hunter and the hunted. With a final terrifying howl the wolf caught its prey and with a giant leap brought them both crashing to the ground!

'Hey! Get off! Your hurting!' came a voice from under a great pile of leaves.

'Grrrr!' came the reply.

Six girls rushed up to view the kill: Sophie, Cressida, Beaky, Lou and the twins Harry and Hen.

'Leaping liquorice! That was brill Susie!' exclaimed Harry to the wolf.

'Leaping liquorice times two. You had me convinced!' added Hen.

The wolf howled one final time and then stood up, pulling twigs out of her fluffy hair. It was Susannah-Sue Whistle-White or Susie as she preferred to be called. She smiled shyly. 'I'm thorry if I frightened you Abby, but I was tho enjoying being the wolf!'

'That's alright,' said Abby getting up and brushing leaves off her red jumper. 'I wouldn't have thought someone as small and timid as you Susie could be so terrifying!'

'But that's what's so good about acting,' said Beaky. 'You can pretend to be people you are not and if you believe it enough you become that person or animal or beast or monster or whatever it is.'

'Like I am small and feeble normally, but if I'm feeling that I really *am* a wolf I become ...'

'Ferocious!' finished Abby for Susie. 'Next time *you* can be *Red Riding Hood* and *I'll* be the wolf. Grrrr!'

It was the Daisy Drama Club's first rehearsal for *Red Riding Hood*. Sophie and Cressida, who were best of best friends and both loved drama, lived in the village of Wissop where there was no drama group or stage school or acting classes or performances of any kind whatsoever. So they had had the brilliant idea of setting up the Daisy Drama Club so they could put on plays themselves and actually *do* some acting instead of *pretending* to do some acting.

Sophie and Cressie had spent a very short time choosing their next play after the drama of their first performance, *A Christmas Carol*.

'I think we should do a fairy story this time. Something that everyone already knows so we can add lots of bits and bobs to make it fun.'

'We need good characters though.'

'And a good baddy.'

'Something hairy and scary,' added Sophie thoughtfully, remembering how Lollipop, Abby's sheepdog, had attacked Mrs Theodora Whistle-White's furry coat at their last performance, thinking the coat was a big hairy beast.

'I'm thinking something wolfee,' added Cressida.

'I'm seeing a red cloak and hood ...'

'... a basket of goodies ...'

'... grannies locked in cupboards ...'

'... woodcutters rushing through forests waving axes ...'

'*Red Riding Hood*!' said the best friends together, knowing exactly what each other was thinking as only best friends do.

And that was that!

Sophie and Cress decided to hold the first rehearsal in Dragon's Wood because:

1) they hadn't got a script yet.

2) they thought it would be a good idea to feel what it is like to rush around dodging in and out of trees which is quite a different feeling from running across an open meadow or up and down pavements or chasing each other around in the playground.

They soon had a list of the problems of running in woods:

Problems of Running in Woods

1. twigs poke at you
2. roots trip you up
3. leaves swirl up from the ground
4. leaves hide rabbit holes so you might fall in and tumble right down and get stuck
5. you can get lost
6. it's super scary running through the trees if you are being chased by a big hairy beast who wants to eat you

The Daisy Drama Club, or DDC as it was called by people in a hurry, had been taking it in turns all morning to play the different characters in *Red Riding Hood*: Red Riding Hood herself, her mother, the wolf, the woodcutter and the granny. They were now puffed out and starvingly hungry. Luckily Sophie's mum had played her part and filled a basket with goodies. The DDC were looking forward to munching away at the gooey chocolate cake and flapjacks.

But when Sophie looked in the basket of goodies she got a terrible shock.

'The goodies! They're gone!'

The gooey chocolate cake and flapjacks had disappeared.

Only a few crumbly little crumbs remained!

'Leaping liquorice! Completely guzzled!' cried Harry.

'Leaping liquorice! Totally gobbled!' added Hen.

Abby's tummy rumbled in disappointment.

'Who could it pothibly be?' asked Susie anxiously.

'It couldn't be any of *us*,' said Beaky tapping her nose thoughtfully. 'We've been working hard together all morning and that was a fantastic amount of chocolate cake to eat quickly and secretly!'

'Anyone who could gobble at *that* speed would be feeling sick now,' added Lou. 'Anyone feeling sick?' Lou looked round suspiciously.

'I don't feel thick but I do feel thcared,' said Susie.

Dragon's Wood seemed darker than before and more threatening.

'I don't like it here anymore!' said Susie getting the creeps. 'Not at all! Pleath can we go home!'

'Look!' shouted Harry.

A small figure in a red coat with a hood crossed the woodland path. She was hurrying along, carrying a basket and was quickly swallowed up by the dense trees.

'Red Riding Hood!' whispered Abby.

'Leaping liquorice! Impossible!' said Harry and Hen together.

There was a blood curdling howl. Out of a bush flew an enormous grey hairy beast. It stopped for an instant, surprised by the girls, then snarled, showing vicious razor-sharp white teeth and bright crimson gums, dripping with saliva. The snarl became a hideous howl then it turned and raced into the woods after the little figure in red.

'Aaaaaaaahh ... the wolf!'
screamed Susie, terrified.

The DDC charged out of Dragon's Wood as fast as they could, tearing down the hill, through the meadows bordering Wissop village, at top speed back up Blacksmith Lane and into the safety of The Barn Theatre, where they sat on the edge of the stage puffing and panting and trying to catch their breath.

Sophie's mum heard them and came into the barn carrying a plate piled high with flapjacks.

'Anybody still hungry?' she asked.

But the DDC were too shocked by what they had seen to even think about eating flapjacks!

'It must have been a mirage,' said Beaky wisely, tapping her nose. 'It happens in the desert when people are desperate for water and their throats are as dry as sandpaper and they cannot walk another step because they are dying of thirst and then, incredibly, they see glittering water on the horizon. On hands and knees they drag themselves desperately towards it but when they get there the water completely disappears. It wasn't really there in the first place.'

'But we didn't see any water,' said Abby. 'We saw Red Riding Hood and a mean and horrible wolf!'

'Precisely! Because we had been *thinking* about Red Riding Hood and a mean and horrible wolf all morning we *thought* we actually *saw* them.'

'What I saw was *real*! I know it was!' said Abby resolutely.

'Can we rehearth in here next time?' asked Susie. 'I don't want to go up to that howwible Dragon's Wood again - ever! ever! ever!'

The Barn Theatre seemed such a friendly place after Dragon's Wood: King Arthur, the Daisy Drama Club's royal patron who had been given to them, along with chairs and stage lights, or lamps as he liked to call them, by Sophie's Uncle Max, were all there; upstairs on the first floor was the lighting gallery, where John, Sophie's brother who was cajoled into being lighting director, would operate from during performances; there was the black curtain hiding the thrillingly secret backstage area; and dotted around were all sorts of odd bits and bobs - the lucky dip barrel, a *TICKET OFFICE* sign, a big chest labelled *PROPS*, an enormously fat christmas turkey made from stuffed tights and a costume rail with a few left over items from *A Christmas Carol* - Scrooge's nightshirt, Marley's chain, Mrs Cratchit's bonnet and, propped up against the wall, little Tiny Tim's crutch. It all made The Barn Theatre exciting and friendly

... and just waiting for a another play.

'We'll rehearse here from now on,' said Sophie.

'But what about the thcwipt?' added Susie. 'We haven't even started that tho we don't know who we are or what we are meant to be saying.'

Everyone turned and looked at Beaky.

Beaky wasn't Beaky's real name but she had a really long pointy nose so everyone called her Beaky. In fact, she was proud of the name *and* the nose because her Grandpa Albert also had a very long nose and everyone said they looked the same which made both of them happy as they were best of friends.

Beaky and Albert were also both mad on reading and scribbling out stories and poems. Albert's house was stuffed full of books and he had helped Beaky write the script for the DDC's *A Christmas Carol*.

'Would you mind ...?' asked Cressida. Writing the script was a big job and she didn't like to ask too much.

'Just have a go at writing the ...' added Sophie.

'... have a go at writing the script - again!' finished Beaky her eyes shining with delight. She tapped her nose, looked about her, then said, 'It would be a great honour!'

Susie gave Beaky a hug.

'You're thuch a thtar Beaky! But,' she added, her voice now serious, 'I do think we need the thcwipt thoon. We've got to thtart learning our lineth and I take ageth and ageth and ageth to learn my lineth and the play is going to be at the end of term isn't it Creth?'

'Yes. Curtain up on the last weekend of term,' agreed Cressida.

'Leaping liquorice! That's only seven weeks away!' said Harry.

'Six,' corrected Cress, handing out the rehearsal timetable.'Could you get the script written for our rehearsal next Saturday Beaky?'

That would require ...

- Super
= Speedy
= Script Writing!

Beaky looked to one side, then tapped her nose and nodded. 'The scripts will be here!'

The Monday Club

On Monday after school Beaky went round to her Grandpa's house, knocked on the door and, when he answered, asked in a loud voice (Grandpa Albert was a little deaf) if Albert could help write the script for the DDC's second play.

Albert was over the moon!

'Another script! Another script! What's it to be?' he yelled, leaping in the air and kicking his heels together in excitement. '*Oliver Twist? Hard Times? Bleak House?*'

'No! Not a Charles Dickens book this time.'

'Not Charles Dickens?'

Albert was incredulous! Amazed! After all Dickens was the best, the greatest, the king of story tellers, with the most marvellous characters and intricate plots and ...

'We're doing *Red Riding Hood*.'

'*Red Riding Hood*?'

'Yes Grandpa. *Red Riding Hood*!' Beaky said as loudly and clearly as she could so that there would be no mistake.

'*Red Riding Hood*! But that's just a fairy story! A nightie-night narrative for the nursery! A tiddler's tale! What's wrong with Dickens?'

'Nothing Grandpa. But *Red Riding Hood* is a good simple story and it's got some brilliant characters.'

'A girl in a red hood? A bossy mother? An ancient old granny? A weedy woodcutter? A greedy guzzling wolf? Not even enough characters for everyone in the Daisy Drama Club!'

'Yes Grandpa ... but we could add in our own *extra* characters! We could be inventive! Imaginative! Creative! Get our minds whirling!'

Albert stopped in his tracks. He tapped his nose, thinking.

'Get our minds whirling! That is the very thing I have been looking for!'

Albert grabbed Beaky's hands and swung her round, doing a little dance on the doorstep, then tapped his nose again.

'Come in Beaky! This is *not* a disaster after all. I have some friends right here who are stuffed with ideas! Weird and wonderful ideas pouring out of them in great puffs of creativity!'

Beaky followed Albert down his long thin hallway, lined each side with bookshelves overflowing with hundreds and thousands of books, and into his kitchen at the back of his little house, and there were five old people sitting round the kitchen table looking sad.

'This,' said Albert to Beaky, 'is the Monday Club.'

'We're called the Monday Club because we meet on Monday which is sad as Monday is the saddest day of the week,' said one old gentleman sadly.

'Monday is the only day we are allowed out of our old people's home, the Battleaxe Barracks,' said a wispy old lady in a breathy way.

'Only allowed out for one hour a week,' said the old gentleman, whose face was all wrinkled up like a walnut.

'But Monday is our happiest day because we *are* allowed out so perhaps we should call it the Friday Club as most people say *Friday* is the happiest day of the week as it's the last day of the week before the weekend,' said a hat and then Beaky realised there was someone under it but he was so small that you could only see his hat above the table.

'Don't be barking mad!' said a sharp woman sharply. 'It's Monday so we can't call it the Friday Club because it's Monday. You simply can't have a Friday Club on a Monday.'

'Yes but you can't have a Monday Club on a Monday if the Monday Club is meant to be happy because everyone knows Monday is the worst day of the week and Friday is the best day so we should call it the Friday Club even though it is a Monday and then we would be happy on Monday.'

'But we *are* happy on Monday.'

'But we *aren't* on Friday because we don't have the Monday Club.'

'Perhaps we should have a sad Monday Club on Friday and a happy Friday Club on Monday.'

'Sorry to interrupt,' said a quiet voice that had not spoken before. 'Could somebody be awfully kind and tell me, is it Tuesday today?'

The group groaned and fell back into silence staring into their tea cups.

After a while the wispy lady with the breathy voice said, 'Strange. My tea leaves are telling me it's Wednesday. But then you can see into the future if you look at your tea leaves so perhaps it *is* Wednesday *in* my tea cup but Monday *out* of it.'

'What happens if you sip a bit of Wednesday?' asked the hat.

'Ah, that would make it Tuesday in your mouth and Monday sort of round you but Wednesday still in your tea cup.'

'I see,' said the hat.

Everyone sighed.

After a while the sharp lady said in a loud shrill voice that made everyone jump, 'It's Thursday today!'

'Can't be the Monday Club then,' said the walnut. 'Unless you mean it's Thursday in your tummy if you have swallowed the tea and it's got a bit ahead of time.'

The kitchen clock struck half past four.

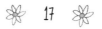

'Dear friends,' said Albert in a loud voice, 'I am sorry to interrupt your philosophical discussion but my granddaughter is here and urgently, desperately needs help writing a script for her play. She's a member of the fantasticalicas Daisy Drama Club and their next performance is going to be a sensational production of *Red Riding Hood* ...

...but there are eight girls in the club and only five parts in the story - the girl in a red hood, a bossy mother, an ancient old granny, a weedy woodcutter and a greedy guzzling wolf. They need your creativity! Your spark! Your ingenuity to think of three other characters to make eight in total - one each!'

There was silence round the table.

'Come on folks!' said Albert loudly. 'You've only got ten minutes before I've got to deliver you home, so let's have some really good ideas.'

The hat peeped over onto the table and saw Albert's pepperpot sitting on the table.

'Pepperpot,' said the hat.

'Possibly,' said Albert doubtfully. 'How do you think we could weave a pepperpot as a character into the story?'

'The granny could be having a sausage sandwich and then she decides to put some pepper on it and the pepper could make her sneeze and then the wolf who is lurking outside might hear her and rush in and gobble her up.'

'Interesting idea,' said Albert. 'Do you think a pepperpot would be an exciting part to perform?'

'You'd have to be pulled up on strings so that the granny could completely tip you upside down like a real pepperpot,' said the hat thoughtfully.

'Birds!' said the sharp lady. 'Bring in birds. They are lively and can fly around and be in and out of any scene you like. That is the trouble with pepperpots. They are severly limited in their movement.'

Beaky tapped her nose. 'Birds' actually *was* a good idea.

'What would you call the birds?' Beaky asked tentatively.

All the old people swivelled their ancient, wrinkly necks and turned to stare at Beaky in surprise as if they hadn't noticed her before - which they hadn't.

'Who are you?' asked the sharp lady sharply.

'This is Beaky my granddaughter who is performing in the play,' said Albert.

'Well why didn't you say so?' said the sharp lady very sharply.

The clock struck quarter to four.

'Bother,' sighed Albert. 'Time to deliver you all back to Battleaxe Barracks.'

'Shame!' said the sharp lady. 'Just as we were starting to have some jolly good ideas!'

'But we mustn't be late!' said the wispy lady in a frightened breathy voice.

'No! We mustn't be late!' the others echoed.

'Miss Gristlegrundelblug will not tolerate lateness!' added the walnut. 'Time for immediate evacuation!'

To Beaky's surprise all the old people jumped up, grabbed their sticks and ran at top speed in a very slow doddering old people's way out of the kitchen, down the book-lined little hallway and climbed into Miranda.

Miranda was a milk float that Albert had bought off Sunny Smiles Dairy when he had stopped being a Sunny Smiles Dairy milkman which was after he had been a soldier, an acrobat, a safari guide, a secret agent, a spy spying on secret agents, a double secret agent spying on spies, a professional scarf knitter, an Olympic gymnast specialising in triple twist, twirling backflip somersaults, a circuit judge and before he had had to retire, which in the end he was glad about because now he was a poet and wrote verse that was admired all over the world.

Albert had taken out all the old milk crates from the open space at the back of Miranda and welded two armchairs and a sofa to the floor which made it a most luxurious ride for passengers. To stop it being too windy a ride he had fixed a curtain at half height so passengers would have warm knees but still be able to admire the view. All in all it was a most comfortable way of travelling.

'Bye Beaky,' waved Albert, putting on his Sunny Smiles Dairy milkman's cap and driving off, whistling. Whistling and wearing the milkman's cap were two habits that he could not shake off when he was at the wheel of Miranda. 'Come round tomorrow and we'll have another go at the script!'

'Bye Grandpa,' said Beaky and she watched Miranda stop and start as she made her way jerkily down the lane to deliver the five old people back to the doorstep of Battleaxe Barracks.

Script Writers

The following day - which was pretty much definitely a Tuesday - Beaky went round to see Grandpa Albert again.

'Come in!' he cried in excitement. 'We have the characters all planned out! Look!'

Albert handed Beaky a very thick piece of paper. The words at the top said ...

'Battleaxe Barracks,
Home for No Hopers
(Ancient Variety)'

... and were printed in black ink and stuck up from the surface of the paper when Beaky ran her finger over them.

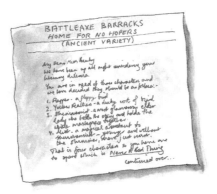

Underneath in very neat joined up writing was written:

My Dear Miss Beaky,

We have been up all night considering your literary dilemma.

You are in need of three characters and we have decided they should be as follows:

1. Flapper - a flappy bird

2. Yellow Feathers - a ducky sort of bird

3. Shimmermist - a most glamourous elder lady who tells the story and holds the whole masterpiece together

4. Mist - a magical assistant to Shimmermist - much younger and without the shimmer, just more mist

That is four characters so you have one spare which is Never A Bad Thing.

We have also decided you should have a chorus as follows:

1. Trees of the Wood - a chorus

The chorus is as many characters as you like so you have lots to spare which is Never

At All A Bad Thing.

We will waive our fee as thinking of these things has given us all much pleasure.

Yours sincerely and most faithfully yours in unison with you who values the world of the capital letter and full stop,

The Battleaxers

(Literary Appreciation Society)

(formed in: very recently).

PS We think you should call Red Riding Hood 'Josephine'. It is far too complicated for Red Riding Hood - the girl - to have the same name as Red Riding Hood - the play. You will get muddled and not be able to think clearly and we are most insistant that you take seriously the subject of thinking. Think! Think! Think!

'Fantasticalicas!' said Albert. 'Aren't their ideas simply *fantasticalicas*!'

'But they have suggested one character too many even if you don't count the chorus,' said Beaky puzzled.

'Oh a minor inconvenience,' said Albert. 'We absolutely *must* use their ideas! Their creativity! Their spark! Their ingenuity!'

'But why?' asked Beaky. 'Couldn't we just think of our own extra characters?'

'My dear Beaky,' said Albert looking serious. 'Thinking about your play has been the most exciting thing that has happened to the residents of Battleaxe Barracks in two hundred and fifty three years. They were sinking into the depths of despondency! The murky mire of old age! The abyss of the end! Your play has brought them back to life.'

'But that's impossible,' said Beaky 'Nobody lives for two hundred and fifty three years.'

'Two hundred and fifty three years if you total up all the years that they have all been at Battleaxe Barracks all together,' explained Albert. 'The thing is Beaky, they are very dear friends and it is such a joy to see a little sparkle coming back into their dull and dreary lives. It's given them the chance to shine again! To share the spotlight!'

Beaky tapped her nose for a second, then she hugged Albert.

'Grandpa, let's do it!' she said firmly.

'Up and away!' cried Albert grinning.

Out came the old typewriter.

Albert fed in a piece of paper and turned to Beaky.

'Right then, what's the first line?'

'The hardest line!' they both said together and burst out laughing.

After that they got down to some serious work and it was with great pride and joy that Beaky left Albert's house several hours later with a finished copy of the script tucked firmly under her arm.

A second copy had been typed up for Albert so he could read it and re-read it and re-read it just incase there were any teeny weeny improvements that could be made - although both Beaky and Albert knew it was absolutely-bally-lootely *PERFECT*.

On her way home Beaky called in at the vicarage where the Right Rev Marbles had a photocopier which was vital to the production of the Wissop Parish News, and made nine extra copies.

Then she dropped one copy, marked *TOP SECRET* off at Sophie's house so that Sophie and Cressida could draw up the cast list before the Saturday morning rehearsal.

Exhausted but elated, Beaky finally got home and fell asleep dreaming of wolves wearing red cloaks and eating pepper cake sprinkled with chocolate.

Cast List Kidnap

On Saturday morning Abby got up early to give herself enough time to catch her mischievous pony, Pickle, groom him so at least some of the brambles were out of his hairy coat and he didn't look like a mobile blackberry bush and also to tell him the exciting news.

'This morning, Pickle, the *Red Riding Hood* cast list is going to be pinned on The Barn Theatre's door and everyone will find out who will be who in the next performance. Bertie is very excited aren't you Bertie!'

Bertie, Abby's pet mouse, who went everywhere with her, was still asleep but she knew he *was* excited by the way his tail was twitching and his little pink nose was sniffling, so she carefully put him in her top pocket without waking him.

Lollipop, the sheepdog, came bounding in.

'Lollipop! I know you are excited too. But you'll have to be on absolute very best behaviour if you are going to come to the performance this time! You caused chaos attacking Mrs Theodora Whistle-White when she was sitting in the audience at *A Christmas Carol*. Yes, I know you thought she was a big bear in her huge furry coat but that is no excuse!'

Lollipop wagged his tale at the memory. He couldn't *wait* to have another go at the big bear!

'Good girl Lollipop,' said Abby. 'I know you'll behave yourself perfectly!'

Pickle was anxious to get to The Barn Theatre, and for a moment stood unusually still so Abby could tack him up quickly and mount without him going round and round in circles.

Ready at last, the little group trotted off at top speed through the village and into the yard at Sophie's house, The Old Farmhouse.

An upstairs window flew open and Sophie, having heard the clip clopping of Pickle, shouted out 'Hi Abby! Cress is here. We'll be down in a sec. We're just finishing off the *Things to Do List (3)*. The cast list is up though, so you can have a look!'

'Ooh, I can't wait!' called back Abby, leaping off Pickle and running over to the huge barn doors with Pickle in tow and Lollipop racing alongside.

There it was! Pinned to the great barn door was a beautifully illustrated cast list.

Abby anxiously ran her eye down the list of characters.

'Where am I? Where am I? Oh look Pickle! I'm Shimmermist! Hang on - who *is* Shimmermist? Oh NO Pickle! Come back! PICKLE!'

CAST LIST

Rose .... Susie
Mother ..... ~~Lou Abe~~ Lou
Grandmama ...... Beaky
Will the Woodcutter... Harry
Shimmermist ..... ~~Abby Lou Abby~~
Mist .... Lou ... (again)
Wolfee .... Hen
Yellow Feathers ... Cress
Flapper .... Sophie

Chorus
Trees of the Wood ... All

Directors ... Sophie
            and Cressida

Prompt .... Beaky
Lighting ..... John

Pickle had been looking at the cast list with Abby and suddenly decided to take a much closer look. He bared his teeth and grabbed a corner and pulled. The list came off. Pickle neighed in delight and trotted out of the yard and off down the road with the cast list in his mouth and Lollipop scampering alongside.

'PICKLE! Come back! You naughty pony! Stop him Lollipop!'

The commotion woke up Bertie who nearly fell out of Abby's top pocket in shock.

'Pickle has stolen the cast list Bertie! Come on! We've got to catch him!'

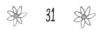

Abby dashed out of the yard. To her relief she saw that Harry and Hen, the twins with the bright red hair, big smiles, freckles and massive front teeth had caught the cheeky pony and were *both* riding him back.

'Hi Abby! Pickle nearly ran us over!'

'We guessed he must have escaped!'

'What has he been eating for breakfast?'

Abby forced open Pickle's mouth and recovered a bedraggled piece of paper.

'It's not breakfast! It's the cast list! We've got to get it back on the barn door before Sophie and Cress realize it's been kidnapped!'

Abby tried to flatten out the piece of paper and did her best to pin it up neatly again. A few edges had been chewed off and the beautiful watercolour illustrations that framed the cast list were smudged.

But Harry and Hen didn't care about that. They were too anxious to see which parts they had been given.

'Yippee! I'm Wolfee!' yelled Hen in delight.

'And I'm Will the Woodcutter!' grinned Harry.

'That means we'll have to fight each other,' said Hen putting up her fists.

'A stage fight!' said the twins with glee and they flew into violent combat.

John, Sophie's brother rushed over to check that Sophie had not landed him with a part without asking him first. 'Phew!' He was on lighting again. At least he could sit up on the first floor of The Barn Theatre and look out for spiders - his favourite pastime.

Beaky, Lou and Susie arrived. They all rushed up to have a look.

Susie was disappointed.

'Who ith Roth?' she asked.

'Rose *is* Red Riding Hood!' explained Beaky. 'I, or that is, someone thought, it was too complicated to have Red Riding Hood as the girl and

Red Riding Hood as the play and this somebody, actually somebodies, suggested we call Red Riding Hood, the girl, Josephine but I did put my foot down at that and thought Rose would be a much better name. So Susie, it looks like Sophie and Cressida have chosen *you* to be Rose ... that is Red Riding Hood!'

'Me! Red Riding Hood! Roth!' shrieked Susie in fear and delight. 'Oh I don't ... *me* in the thpotlight! ... I couldn't pothibly ... oh I might ... oh thank you!'

Susie was over the moon. When she had first joined the DDC she had been as shy as a mouse too scared to sniff at the finest cheese. Now Sophie and Cressida thought she was good enough to play Rose!

'What is Shimmermist?' asked Abby.

'Shimmermist,' explained Beaky, going all floaty and wobbly, 'is a mysterious character who shimmers in the mist and tells the story in a magical mysterious way.'

Abby looked unconvinced. She was more at home on ponies than shimmering mistily about the stage ...

'It's odd that we have more extra characters than people,' said Lou. 'Look, I'm Mother *and* Mist.'

'That's because there *are*,' said Beaky. It was too hard to explain right now about *The Battleaxers (Literary Appreciation Society)*.

'How are you going to be Grandmama *and* the

prompt, Beaky?' asked Susie. 'What if you forget your own lineth? How will you be able to prompt yourthelf if you're on thtage yourthelf?'

Beaky tapped her nose and thought for a moment.

'I will just have to make sure I *don't* forget. And if I do I will just have to improvise - make it up as I go along!'

'Oh Beaky, you're tho *brave*!' said Susie in admiration.

Just then Sophie and Cressida came out of the house with their *Things To Do List (3)*. It had taken them all Friday evening to cast the play and they were anxious that some people would not be as happy as others about their part so they had stayed up in Sophie's bedroom and peeped out of her window as everyone had the chance to have a look at the cast list.

'It's not spying,' said Cressida. 'It's simply avoiding confrontation.'

One thing they had missed though was Pickle's cast list kidnap! But Abby didn't know this and was horrified to hear Cressie point at the list and cry in astonishment,

'Look!'

'That's impossible!' said Sophie dumbfounded.

'I can explain,' mumbled Abby unhappily. 'You see Pickle ...'

'Those pictures round the edge - of trees and baskets of goodies and a hairy wolf,' said Cressida, 'were not there when we pinned up the list an hour ago!'

'Who could have drawn them?' asked Sophie amazed. 'They're so good. But why is the list so soggy and smudged?'

'The soggy smudgy bit was Pickle's fault I'm afraid,' said Abby guiltily. 'But I promise he didn't do the drawings, did you Pickle?'

Pickle shook his head.

'Who could have drawn them then?' said Beaky. 'It must have been *somebody*!'

'I hope there are not going to be thpooky goingth-on like at our latht performance,' said Susie nervously.

'We don't have time for spooky goings-ons,' said Lou. 'We need to get on with our rehearsals!'

Sophie and Cressida *were* totally baffled by the drawings. But, like best friends always do, they both thought the same - and that was they simply didn't have time for distractions now. There was a show to put on. They would have to investigate the *Mystery of the Appearing-From-Nowhere-Illustrations* later.

'Have you got the rest of the scripts Beaky?' asked Cressida.

Beaky tapped her nose and her bag.

'All here!' she said proudly, taking out the remaining eight scripts, one for each of the cast and one for John.

Susie, forgetting all about 'thpooky goingth-on' turned and hugged Beaky, adding, 'Beaky, you really are a thtar!'

The First Read Through

The excitement of casting over, the Daisy Drama Club sat down in The Barn Theatre on Uncle Max's chairs, and, under the watchful eye of King Arthur, read *Red Riding Hood adapted by Albert and Beaky*, right through from Act 1 Scene 1 to the final finale.

Susie got into the part of Rose stupendously especially in the scenes with her stage mother. It was strangely like being with her *own* mother, the formidable Mrs Theodora Whistle-White:

```
MOTHER Rose, take Grandmama
    This basket of goodies.
    It's filled with the latest
    Granny Cold Survival Kit!

ROSE Granny Cold Survival Kit?
    Let's have a look at it.
```

Mother pulls out a long string of items from the basket: underwear, sausages, kettles, etc.

```
ROSE Mother dearest,
    This kit should do the trick
    And stop poor Grandmama feeling sick.

MOTHER Well my heroine don't delay.

ROSE No! No! I'll leave straight away.
```

Exit Rose

```
MOTHER (calling) Rose! Rose! Rose! Come back!
```

Enter Rose

MOTHER You can't go off into the wood
    Without your red cloak and hood.

Mother puts red cloak with hood onto Rose.

MOTHER Just give me a twirl
    My gorgeous little girl.

Rose gives a twirl

    Oh don't you look a treat.
    Doesn't she look sweet?
    Now off you go, my little Red Riding Hood.
    Quick! Quick! This is no time for fun.
    Run, girl! RUN!

Exit Rose stage right, running.

Exit Mother, stage left.

SHIMMERMIST So off Rose went
    With the Granny Cold Survival Kit
    To save her dear Grandmama
    And make her fighting fit!

'Leaping liquorice!' said Harry when they had finished the whole play. 'That was brill.'

'Leaping liquorice!' added Hen. 'Brill!'

'You were brill Susie,' said Cressida kindly.

'Oh it wath eathy!' said Susie modestly. 'I jutht imagined that Lou my thtage mother wath my *real* mother - ethpecially when I had to put on the red cloak and hood and give a twirl. It'th exactly the thort of thing my mother would make me do - tho embarathing!'

'Beaky, what exactly is the *Granny Cold Survival Kit*?' asked Abby, puzzled.

'Just lots of things tied onto a long string like sausages, knickers, a handkerchief, socks. It can be anything you like so long as it makes the audience laugh,' said Beaky.

'But why would those things be a *Granny Cold Survival Kit*?' asked Abby, persisting. 'I just can't see *how* it would make a granny survive a cold.'

'It's meant to be funny!' said Beaky, impatiently.

'Oh.' Abby was not very imaginative and just could not understand what Beaky meant. But Harry and Hen did.

'Could *we* be in charge of props this time?' asked Harry.

Cress looked at Sophie and Sophie looked at Cress and nodded. It was great to have people volunteering.

'Tip top!' said Hen. 'I can think of some great things to put on the *Granny Cold Survival Kit*!'

'Well I'm glad you two get it!' said Beaky tapping her nose and looking at Abby.

Abby was still looking perplexed.

'If Pickle is ill I give him medicine not things on a string!'

'Oh really Abby!' said Beaky. 'Just try and use your imagination a teeny weeny bit!'

'I can uth my imagination,' said Susie. 'I can imagine in five weeks time we will be performing right here in front of a packed audience. Juth like last time. It wath tho exciting!'

'I vote we start making posters then,' said Lou who liked to be organised. 'And what about costumes?'

'Costumes are on our *Things to Do List (4)*,' said Cressida.

'Lou, would you be wardrobe mistress again?' asked Sophie.

Lou beamed. 'I would be delighted!' she said, already imagining her sewing machine whirring away, the snip, snip of her pinking shears as they zigzagged through a velvet material, the delight of searching through her store of jam jars filled with brightly coloured threads - crimson, emerald green, sapphire, the hunt for that special button - would it be pearl? or shell? or sparkly silver? - and how about the final touches of gold braid, glittering sequins, satin ribbons - perhaps a lacy trim?

The costumes for *Red Riding Hood* would be magnificent!

Lou looked over to the costume rail and in her mind's eye she fabulous costumes hanging there, neatly arranged : the hairy wolfee outfit, a silky red cloak, a funny old grandma's cap.

But what *exactly* would they look like?

What about Shimmermist? And Mist? And Yellow Feathers? And Flapper?

It wasn't just *making* the costumes. They needed to be *designed* as well. With so much to do she might need some help ...

'If everyone could bring a drawing to our next rehearsal of what they think their costume would look

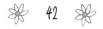

like I'll make a book of designs and then get cracking straight away,' she suggested.

'Oh no!' said Abby. 'I'm terrible at drawing and my costume is the hardest. I have absolutely *no idea* what it will look like and even if I did I couldn't draw it!'

'Just let your *imagination* go wild!' said Lou, Abby thought not at all helpfully.

'Can I just say I do have a bit of imagination. And what's more I'll have to if I'm going to be Shimmer-whatsit. My part needs the most imagination out of everyone in the whole play.'

Sophie and Cressida exchanged glances. Perhaps casting Abby of all people as Shimmermist was a terrible mistake.

'Let's practise the woodland creatures chant again,' suggested Beaky. 'We really need to get some much better sound effects than we did just now. It sounded a bit weedy - not at all what I had imagined.' Beaky tapped her nose and looked at Abby who looked crossly back.

'Good idea,' said Cressida. 'Whenever Rose says *'this place is full of the weirdest woodland creatures'* we all have to make a sound.'

'What sort of sound?'

'A weird woodland creature sort of sound.'

 43

'Like howling or growling or ...'

'Roaring!'

'Hissing!'

'Cheeping!'

'Exactly!'

'And do we *all* do the chant when it says 'All', Beaky?'

'Yes. Whatever your part is you say it, even if you are backstage.'

'Let's try,' said Sophie.

So all the DDC chanted:

```
Creatures of the woodland
Creatures of the wild
Hoooowwwwwwlllll!
```

'Wait a sec! That's terrible! We need to make it more mysterious,' said Sophie. 'Let's try a loud whisper for '*creatures of the woodland*' and then a big howl!'

The DDC tried again:

```
Creatures of the woodland
Creatures of the wild
Hoooowwwwwwlllll!

With screeches and howls,
With screeches and howls,
```

```
From den and burrow,
From nest and hive,
Let's hear that you're ALIVE!
WOODLAND CREATURES!

Howl! Growl! Cheep! Chirp! Hiss!
```

'I've had an idea,' said Abby. 'Those howls still sounded totally feeble. Why don't we get the audience to join in and make howlee sort of noises? Then it will be really loud!'

Everyone stared at Abby.

That was a brilliant idea!

'We could put little pieces of paper on their seats when they arrive so that they know what noise to make,' she added, 'just in case they don't have much *imagination* and can't think of anything!'

Beaky tapped her nose. 'Tiptop Abby! What a krrracker of an idea!'

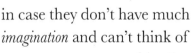

The rest of the morning was spent making three posters and forty tickets and chanting the Trees of the Wood chorus:

```
We are the Trees of the Wood
Some are bad and some are good!
We are the Trees of the Wood
Some are bad and some are good!

I'm very beautiful.
I'm very strong.
I'm very l ... l ... long!
I'm very bendy.
I can sing a song ... La!

We are the Trees of the Wood
Some are bad and some are good!
We are the Trees of the Wood
Some are bad and some are good!

I'm very, very tall.
And I'm the smallest of them all.
If you climb me you might fall ...
I ah ... ah ... ah.. SNEEZE
And I have trouble with ... buzzzzz ... bees!

We are the Trees of the Wood
Some are bad and some are good!
We are the Trees of the Wood
Some are bad and some are good! YEAH!
```

Red Riding Hood rehearsals had got off to a pretty good start!

Mystery Artist

During Monday morning break at Wissop School Sophie and Cressida put up the three posters for *Red Riding Hood*: one outside the gym, one outside the library and one outside the dining room.

Cressida noticed that the new girl, whose name was Alice, had been standing staring at the poster they had pinned up by the gym. She had her hands on her hips and had screwed up her nose as if the poster stank. Obviously she did not like the look of the poster at all. Suddenly she said, 'Rubbish! Total rubbish!' and stomped off!

When Cressida passed the poster at lunchtime someone had drawn a border all round the edge. To begin with Cressida was shocked that their poster had been vandalised - but then she felt pleased. The border was wonderful! A woodcutter was chasing a wolf who was chasing Rose. She had to admit, it did look much better.

Hurriedly Cressida ran off to find Sophie. Just as they were about to go and have a look together the bell rang and they had to go into their double maths lesson with the fearsome Miss Guffy - and you did not dare to be late for Miss Guffy. It was not until the end of the afternoon that they got to the gym to see the poster. Sophie was impressed.

'Who could it be? Let's have a look at the posters outside the library and the dining room.'

But the poster from outside the library had gone!

'I can't believe that someone would have taken it down!' said Sophie dismayed.

'What about the poster outside the dining room?'

It too had completely disappeared!

Vanished into thin air!

'We'll just have to make some more and bring them in tomorrow,' said Cressida philosophically.

'Double disaster!' said Sophie 'We've already got heaps and heaps and heaps of homework to do.'

But the next day when they went into school to put up their new rather hurriedly made posters they were in for another shock.

Outside the library and the dining room were beautifully illustrated posters already up on the wall advertising *Red Riding Hood*!

On the library poster there was a naturalistic border of trees and leaves and at the bottom there was a little path running through a wood down to a stream where there were seven stepping stones.

'The Seven Dwarfs!' said Sophie and Cress together in amazement.

The Seven Dwarfs were seven stepping stones that crossed the stream in Dragon's Wood. The illustration looked exactly the same!

On the dining room poster the border had been decorated with all sorts of goodies that you might take in a picnic basket if you were visiting a poorly granny. There were apples and sandwiches ... but even more mysteriously, gooey chocolate cake and flapjacks!

'It must be Lou,' said Sophie. 'She's good at drawing. Let's ask her.'

But Lou who enjoyed art nearly as much as sewing was amazed when she saw the posters.

'I might be quite good at drawing but not that good!' she said impressed. 'I wonder who it could be?'

The new girl Alice came stomping down the corridor. She saw the three girls looking at the dining room poster and turned and shot off in the opposite direction.

But Lou had spotted her.

'Hey! Alice!' she called and ran after her, Sophie and Cressida following.

They raced round the corner and crashed straight into Miss Guffy, who was carrying twenty text books. The books went flying. The girls helped Miss Guffy pick up the books and by the time they had finished Alice had vanished.

Witches and Hobgoblins

Dragon's Wood was one of those places that sometimes looked bright and beautiful and sometimes hairy scary. After the fright of their first rehearsal Sophie and Cressida felt a bit cautious about returning but they desperately wanted to see how closely the illustration of the stepping stones on the poster matched the real place.

So after school they set off through Scarraway Meadow along the grassy track to Dragon's Wood planning to go down to the Seven Dwarfs, the seven stepping stones which enabled travellers to cross Badger's Brook.

It was bright and sunny as they set off but black clouds soon gathered and it felt stormy by the time they reached the wood.

'I really do feel like Red Riding Hood in the forest now,' said Sophie.

The trees seemed to encircle them, green fingers leaning down and poking their faces.

A monkjack deer leapt out in front of them and both girls squeaked with a sudden rush of fear.

Boldly, but not feeling very bold, they made their way down the path to Badger's Brook.

'Look,' said Sophie, pointing at the water and the seven shiny wet stepping stones that formed a line from the near bank to the far bank. 'The Seven Dwarfs. *Exactly* like the illustration on the poster.'

A water vole splashed as it leapt into the bubbling brook and the girls jumped.

'Ooh! What is it today? Why is it so creepy here?' whispered Cressida, trying to feel brave.

And then they both saw it.

A hooded red figure crouching by the water, bent over, stirring a pot of dark, evil looking liquid.

And worse, a big hairy creature was lurking in the trees just beyond.

Sophie and Cress froze.

Who could they be?

A witch stirring her lotions and potions?

A hairy scary wolf?

It was getting dark.

An owl shrieked.

The sudden noise sent the girls dashing - one, two, three, four, five, six, seven! - over the Seven Dwarfs, and up the path the other side.

Cress glanced back but to her surprise the figure had completely disappeared.

The girls raced out of Dragon's Wood and back onto Blacksmith Lane, which wound its way through Wissop village.

Once on the lane they felt safer and slowed down to catch their breath.

'Stop right there!' came a sharp voice from the hedgerow. 'What a hurry you're in and just when I need some help.'

The girls panting from their sprint turned to see an ancient old face staring at them from out of the hornbeam hedge. Who could it be ...

... a witch?

  ... a horrible hag?

    ... a hobgoblin?

      ... a prehistoric crone?

'What are you staring at you poky faced girls. I'll tell your mothers and fathers and aunties and uncles and your doddery old grandparents and your even older more doddery great-grandparents that you have NO MANNERS!'

'It's Miss Windrush,' whispered Sophie to Cress. 'I met her once when she knocked on our door to see if we had any spare plums or apples or pears going. She is the most ancient person in the village, at least one hundred and fifty years old according to John and as evil tempered as a hornet in a jam jar!'

'What's that? What are you saying?' snapped Miss Windrush sharply.

'Sorry Miss Windrush. You made us jump.'

'Don't speak so loudly! I'll be caught!' For a second Miss Windrush looked nervous. Then she recovered.

'You been down at the Seven Dwarfs?' she asked sharply, crinkling up her face and speaking in that voice that says it's a Very Bad Idea to go to the Seven Dwarfs. 'Did you see anything creepy? Anything a bit spooky wooky that sent cold fingers running up and down your spine?'

'Was it you there just now?' asked Cressida cautiously.

'Me? Of course not you numbskull nitwit! I'm here aren't I? So I couldn't be there if I'm here!'

Miss Windrush stuck out a bony old hand.

'You've come to help me out, haven't you dearies.'

'Help you out?'

'But how?'

'Help me out of this hedge of course! I'm stuck. I fell in while I was foraging on the other side and my head came right through and now it's stuck!'

Miss Windrush wriggled her scrawny old neck and rolled her head round so far that for a second Sophie and Cress thought it was going to go right round three hundred and sixty degrees.

Both girls wanted to run, but they could not leave the old lady stuck in a hedge, not even the ghastly Miss Windrush, so they grabbed hold of her bony old hands and pulled and pushed and eventually the witchy old hag popped out like a cork.

Instead of saying thank you Miss Windrush demanded snappily, 'Get my basket. It's stuck in the hedge too. And hurry!'

Sophie and Cress poked around in the hedge until they found the basket and pulled it out.

'What are you doing? You're spilling all the nettles!'

Cressida was carefully tipping out the nettles from the basket.

'Sorry,' said Cress. 'It was full of all sorts of stinging nettles!'

'That's our supper! Nettle soup. We don't get much to eat where I live at Battleaxe Barracks! Oh no! So I have to make extra!' snapped Miss Windrush and grabbed the basket off Cressida. 'Now get my stick! There! There! In the bush! Not that twig! My stick! Hurry! Hurry! I have to get back before Miss Gristlegrundelblug notices I'm missing.'

'Missing? Aren't you allowed to come out whenever you like?'

'What a nitwit question! Why do you think it's called Battleaxe Barracks? We're locked in *she* says for our own good! But I escape and forage for nettles and elders and wild garlic - and I use dandelion roots

to make my own coffee. Delicious! Now find my stick! I must get back before Miss Gristlegrundelblug goes on the warpath!'

Sophie found a stick that looked like any old stick, not a proper walking stick and handed it to Miss Windrush.

Miss Windrush snatched it off her. She was about to say something sharp and then paused.

'Thank you dearies. I'm not exactly what you think I am. I just seem to be mean and nasty and as snappy as a crocodile but I'm not really. And something exciting has happened. Very exciting! Which makes me feel all happy inside and not at all snappy! Oh no! Goodnight and don't let the crocodiles BITE!'

And Miss Windrush hurried off up the lane muttering to herself.

But WHAT she was muttering would have surprised Sophie and Cressida if they had been able to hear:

```
We are the Trees of the Wood,
Some are bad and some are good!
We are the Trees of the Wood,
Some are bad and some are good! Yeah!
```

Now it really *was* dark. A tawny owl screeched. Some poor creature out in the wood screamed as Mr Fox caught it in his sharp white teeth.

Sophie and Cress ran!

Susie in the Spotlight

Mrs Theodora Whistle-White was ecstatic!

'My daughter Susannah-Sue has the lead part in a play! She's going to be a star! An actress dazzling in the spotlight of fame!' she told the butcher, the baker, Mr Gumtree at Gumtree Stores, her hairdresser, a policeman who was chasing a burglar, a burglar who was being chased by a policeman, Aunt Agnes from Australia, a newborn baby who gurgled in delight, an apple in her fruit bowl, herself in the mirror, a traffic warden giving her a parking ticket, a dog walker taking three dogs for a walk, three dogs being taken for a walk by a dog walker, a garden gnome, Miss Windrush who she saw in a hedge, Tim Stack who was herding the cows at Farmer Bagwash's farm, a herd of cows being herded by Tim Stack at Farmer Bagwash's farm, Farmer Bagwash who was walking Lollipop, an oak tree and a trout from the fishmongers. The only person she did *not* tell was Lollipop, just in case Lollipop should think about coming along to the performance and attack her furry coat again which would quite spoil Susannah-Sue's moment of glory.

Not only did she tell everyone but she insisted that Susannah-Sue practised her lines every night until she was word perfect. This was good and bad: Susie was already one hundred and fifty percent embarrassed by her mother's behaviour and although she knew her lines (which was good) she was already fed up with her lines (which was bad). In fact it was so bad that by the time the next rehearsal came she decided that being Rose - the lead part! - was the worst thing that had ever happened to her.

Not surprisingly the rehearsal on Saturday was a disaster.

'Susie, that was terrible!' said Sophie after they had rehearsed scene one and before she could stop herself. 'You looked as if you didn't even want to be on the stage let alone acting a character.'

'That's juth it. I *don't* want to be on the thtage anymore,' retorted Susie crying. 'I hate acting and I'm giving up. I'm leaving the DDC right now and no-one can thtop me! I'm going home!'

Susie stormed out!

The DDC watched her in amazement. What could have happened?

'If she wants to go she'll have to go,' said Sophie. 'We can't have people throwing temper tantrums. It's not professional.'

After the rehearsal Cressida found Susie still standing at the gate waiting for her mother.

'I thought you were going home Susie,' Cressida said kindly.

'I was but my mother says I am too young to walk home on my own so I'm waiting and waiting and waiting here for her.'

'I'm sorry you don't want to be Rose anymore,' said Cressida. 'You seemed really excited about it when we put up the cast list.'

'I was,' said Susie. 'But my mother ...'

That was the clue Cressida had been waiting for.

Cressie knew Mrs Theodora Whistle-White was a formidable mother who was convinced her little Susannah-Sue would become a famous actress and that, thought Cressie, was *not* what the DDC was all about.

'Has she been telling everyone about your starring role?' guessed Cressie.

Susie sniffed and nodded.

'She's just proud of you.'

'Yeth but why does she have to make such a big thing of it! It's not ath if I've won an Othcar or anything. It's just a little play, in a little village with a little catht - and I'm very little too.'

'But that's just it Susie,' said Cressie. 'It is only a

small play but that doesn't mean to say it can't be a really good play with good actors! And I think you *are* really good.'

'Do you?'

'Of course I do! Why else would we have given you the lead part! Perhaps one day you *will* win an Oscar!'

'That's what mum keeps saying and it's tho embarathing. I like acting but I don't actually want to *be* an actreth, caught in the thpotlight of fame! I actually want to be a forenthic detective but my mother would be very croth if I told her. She doethn't like dead thingth.'

'She's just proud of you Susie. And quite rightly. Don't let it stop you doing your best in anything - even acting. You are a very important member of the Daisy Drama Club you know. We couldn't do without you.'

Susie smiled. 'I do enjoy it. It'th jutht not necetharily my career.'

'So you'll be back next week?'

A sudden high pitched voice called out 'Darling are you ready? Where's the leading lady? The glamorous girl of the stage! The star in the spotlight!'

It was Susie's mother.

Susie and Cressida looked at one another and Susie giggled.

Now Susie had shared her worry with Cress it didn't seem so bad. '*Yes*,' she thought, 'I will make my mother proud.'

Why not!

'Thee you next week Crethie,' said Susie as she was swept away in her mother's big furry coat.

A Leafy Shock!

At school on Monday morning Beaky found a mysterious note on her desk.

It was from Grandpa Albert.

Dear Beaky,

 Please come round as soon as possible after school.
 There is something I need to show you.
 Be here by 16.30 latest.
  Your loving
  Grandpa

   xxxxxx

Beaky could not concentrate all day and after school raced round to Albert's house. Albert was waiting on the doorstep. He beckoned to her as soon as he saw her.

'Hurry Beaky! Hurry! We have no time to lose.'

What could it be? Beaky followed Albert down the book-lined hallway to the kitchen door which was closed. That was unusual.

Albert knocked on the door.

'Are you ready?' he shouted.

'Ready and waiting,' shouted back a deep voice.

Albert opened the door ...

...BEAKY COULD NOT BELIEVE HER EYES!!!! ...

Standing round Albert's kitchen table were ...

... *FIVE TREES!*

The five trees began to move and sway and then,
to Beaky's amazement, the five trees began to chant
and sing:

```
We are the Trees of the Wood,
Some are bad and some are good!
We are the Trees of the Wood,
Some are bad and some are good!
```

One by one they added a line:

```
I'm very beautiful.
I'm very strong.
I'm very l ... l ... long!
```

 66

```
I'm very bendy.
I can sing a song ... La!
```

Then all together again:

```
We are the Trees of the Wood,
Some are bad and some are good!
We are the Trees of the Wood,
Some are bad and some are good!
```

Then one by one:

```
I'm very, very tall.
And I'm the smallest of them all.
If you climb me you might fall ...
I ah ... ah ... ah.. SNEEZE
And I have trouble with ... buzzzzz ... bees!
```

Then all together again:

```
We are the Trees of the Wood,
Some are bad and some are good!
We are the Trees of the Wood,
Some are bad and some are good! YEAH!
```

After 'YEAH!' the trees bowed and curtseyed in the kitchen as best they could.

'Splendid! Marvellous! Fantasticalicas!' yelled Albert clapping and clapping. 'Weren't they absolutely fantasticalicas, Beaky?'

Beaky was so surprised she could not speak.

They *were* splendid! Marvellous! Fantasticalicas!...

... but who were they and *why* where they doing the Trees of the Wood chorus from the Daisy Drama Club's *Red Riding Hood* script?

As Albert's enthusiastic applause faded away the trees sat down around the little kitchen table and took off their top branches.

'Hello Beaky,' said the wispy lady with the breathy voice. 'Remember us? The Monday Club.'

'We enjoyed your script for *Red Riding Hood*,' said the sharp lady snappily. 'And we want to be in your play.'

Beaky could not believe her ears.

'It would make us very happy,' said the hat.

'Much happier then we have been for years,' said the tree who normally never spoke.

'We have it all planned,' said the walnut.

'See,' said Albert. 'Isn't it marvellous Beaky! Your play has brought the Monday Club back to life!'

Beaky tapped her nose anxiously.

'But Grandpa - what will the DDC say? I mean they don't *know* about the Monday Club.'

'What? You mean you didn't tell your fellow performers that *our* ideas were *our* ideas?' snapped the sharp lady sharply.

'I didn't think ...' began Beaky.

'No you didn't think,' said the hat. 'I didn't used to think and it got me in a lot of trouble.'

'But how would you get to rehearsals?' asked Beaky.

'We don't need to go to rehearsals,' said the walnut. 'We've practised it all already.'

'You see,' said the hat. 'You weren't thinking then were you, otherwise you would have thought that we don't need to come to rehearsals. We know it already.'

'But how will you get to the performance?' asked Beaky. 'I didn't think you were allowed out except on Mondays.'

'We would escape,' said the sharp lady sharply.

'Stuff things in our beds to look like bodies.'

'Tie sheets together and climb out of windows.'

'And we've got disguises.'

'What sort of disguises?' asked Beaky feeling she was nearly beaten.

'Think!' said the hat. 'You definitely are not thinking now. Look our disguises are right under your nose! Trees of course! If anyone spotted us we could just stand still as trees! Trees of the Wood!'

And with that they were off again.

```
We are the Trees of the Wood,
Some are bad and some are good!
We are the Trees of the Wood,
Some are bad and some are good! YEAH!
```

'So what do you think Beaky?' asked Albert.

'I ... I ...' Beaky could not think what to say.

'She's stumped for words!' said the hat.

The Monday Club burst into laughter.

'*Stumped* for words!'

'Ha! Ha! Ha!'

'*Stumped* for words!'

'Hee! Hee! Hee!'

Poor Beaky heard herself saying, 'I think it's a fantasticalicas idea.'

'That's fixed then!' said the sharp lady sharply.

The Monday Club cheered and Beaky just wondered how on earth she was going to break the news to the rest of the Daisy Drama Club!

Paint, Flats, Hammers and Saws

One of the things on Cress's *Things to Do List (9)* was:

Scenery 1) make scenery
          2) Put it uP.

Sophie and Cress were standing in The Barn Theatre, thinking. The stage looked bare. At the back was a black curtain which gave them a backstage, but apart from that they had no scenery yet, whatsoever.

'We could have a back-drop painted to look like a wood,' suggested Cress.

'And how about a sort of stand up thing that you could open up and it would look like Grandmama's cottage inside.'

'And we could make a cupboard out of cardboard boxes that Wolfee could lock Grandmama in.'

So a white sheet was hung across the back of the stage and Sophie and Cress got John to help them paint a woodland scene.

'You know all about insects,' said Sophie to her brother. You might be able to add in those little details that would make it look more realistic.'

Paint was soon flying everywhere ...

... but painting on to the floppy sheet was almost impossible.

Just then Uncle Max drove into the yard, took one look at what they were up to and drove off again.

He was back in half an hour with his trailer and lots of long thin sticks of wood.

The artists were still battling with the floppy back-drop, splattering paint everywhere.

'Stop right there!' said Uncle Max in his commanding theatrical voice. 'You need to make some flats.'

'Flats?' asked Sophie.

'Yes. Theatrical scenery.'

Once upon a time Uncle Max had been a woodcutter in Bavaria. He left when a romantic episode went tragically wrong. Nobody knew the full story as every time someone tried to ask him Uncle Max's glasses steamed up and he got a chokey voice and he would rush out of the room. After the Bavarian calamity he joined the props department of a distinguished theatre in England because he knew all about wood and was very good at sawing. After a few years backstage he knew everything about making props. And after a few more years at the theatre he knew everything theatrical about everything theatrical - even acting. One night when the lead part for *Romeo and Juliet* was ill, and the understudy too faint with nerves to go on stage, Uncle Max had volunteered. The director was desperate as the curtain was about to go up. Uncle Max knew all the lines from watching so many rehearsals so the director allowed him to take the part and, as the reviews raved next day, Uncle Max was magnificent.

'I have never seen a Juliet with such a splendid beard!' wrote one.

After that Uncle Max spent half his time on stage and half his time backstage.

'To make flats,' he explained, 'you start by making a frame. This long thin stick of wood, called a batten, can make the top rail, these two battens the stiles which are the sides of the frame. Then we need all sorts of bits and pieces to make the toggles which will run between the stiles and corner blocks to join the corners.'

'Sounds complicated,' said Sophie.

'Not complicated, just a complicated way of saying lets make a frame then attach your material to it - it will make it much easier to paint and will stop it blowing around and wobbling when you are performing. Don't want the audience to think there is a force twelve hurricane going on backstage do you?'

Uncle Max was soon busy sawing, chipping and hammering.

An hour later two flats were up at the back of the stage and the artists were finding their job much easier. John, who was as mad on insects as Sophie and Cress were mad on drama, enjoyed himself, painting lots of little creepy crawlies creeping about all over the place.

'We were thinking of making a sort of stand up thing that you could open and inside would be Grandmama's cottage,' said Sophie to Uncle Max.

'That sounds like three panels hinged together. I'll get on making the frames for that while you keep painting!'

Uncle Max hummed happily to himself as he sawed and hammered and measured and sawed and hammered a bit more.

By the end of the afternoon the flats were finished and Uncle Max had made three panels and hinged them together so they could be opened and closed.

'All we need now is a big cardboard box to make the cupboard to lock Grandmama in.'

'Unless we just cut a window in one of the panels and she could stick her head through there,' suggested John.

'Chippy idea!' said Uncle Max and within seconds a hole was created. 'Time to get drawing. Rough out the outlines of everything in Grandmama's cottage before you start painting any detail.'

This was a good idea but not that easy to do.

'The fireplace looks like a dustbin,' said Cressie.

'And the rocking chair looks more like a horse,' said Sophie.

'I think my cupboard looks like a coffin,' added John critically.

'I'm exhausted!' said Sophie.

'Time for tea!' said John who was always hungry.

'Let's tidy up the paints and put out fresh water so when we are ready we can get going again straight away,' suggested Cressida.

'And thanks Uncle Max!' said all three in chorus.

'A pleasure,' said Uncle Max beaming under his massive beard. 'Working in the theatre world is always the greatest joy! I'm glad to see your royal patron is still in action!'

'Yes. You make sure nobody comes and steals our scenery, King Arthur,' said Sophie as she closed the barn doors and they all went over to The Old Farmhouse kitchen to see if mum had any goodies to munch.

Revolution!

Thanks to Cressida, Susie decided she *was* going to love performing her part, however embarrassing her mother would be. She was looking forward to the next rehearsal and promised herself that she would apologise to Sophie for being so unprofessional.

Unfortunately on Saturday morning Mrs Theodora Whistle-White had booked a hair appointment for Susie.

'Susie is a star in the making,' Mrs Whistle-White had cooed to the top hair stylist at the salon. 'Make her look a sensation!'

So when Susie did not turn up to the rehearsal on Saturday Sophie felt sick with worry. She had felt guilty all week about being angry with Susie.

Had Susie really left the DDC?

But just in time Susie burst into The Barn Theatre, climbed onto the stage and apologised for being late, for being unprofessional last week and for her ringlets and curls and ribbons and bows!

'Thank goodness!' thought Sophie. Running a drama club was much trickier than she had thought it would be. But at least Susie was back and it would probably be a good idea to apologise for shouting at her, so Sophie said, 'Sorry I was cross, Susie.'

'That's all right, Thophie,' said Susie. 'It mutht be hard for you and Crethie to have to deal with temperamental actretheth. I actually think you are the betht directorth any catht could wish for.'

It was a generous speech and Sophie vowed to herself that she would never be cross with Susie again - at least she would try!

Everyone thought the flats at the back of the stage looked very convincing.

'You'd think you really were in a wood!' said Susie, 'ethpecially with all thoth little creepy crawlieth creeping everywhere!'

'We have still got to paint the indoors of Grandmama's cottage,' explained Cressida, standing behind the folded panels, 'which will open like this.'

Cressida and Sophie opened the triple flats and everyone gasped.

 79

'Leaping liquorice! That's incredible!' said Harry.

'Leaping liquorice! Amazing!' added Hen.

Sophie and Cressida turned and looked at the inside of the flaps and it was *their* turn to be amazed. Someone had completed the inside - and beautifully!

'Ooh!' said Lou. 'I do believe I could actually sit in that rocking chair!'

'I can almost hear the grandfather clock ticking!'

'And the fire crackling!'

'And the kettle whistling!'

'And the cat purring!'

'And that little mouse down by the mouse hole squeaking!'

'I can't believe it!' said Cress.

'We only painted the outline!' said Sophie.

'So who finished it off?' asked Cress.

'Look here's a note.'

I love to paint and draw. Hope you don't mind.

Suddenly there was a barking and howling outside.

'Lollipop!' shouted Abby and she rushed out to see Lollipop fighting a great grey wolfhound.

'Lollipop come here!'

Lollipop feeling outclassed ran over to Abby and cowered behind her. To Abby's surprise the wolfhound bounded into the barn, straight past Lollipop and ran backstage.

'Come back!' shouted Abby and she raced after him. Backstage to her amazement she saw the dog licking a girl in a red duffle coat who was patting him and trying to calm him down.

'What are you doing here?' asked Abby.

The girl looked furious at being found and for a second Abby thought she was about to escape.

Abby grabbed her arm.

'What are you doing here?' Abby repeated.

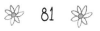

The girl looked defiant, shook Abby off and marched onto the stage.

Everyone gasped.

It was Alice, the new girl at school.

'So you've found me and all I can say is I'm sorry. And that's it!'

She crossed her arms and stood there staring at everyone, angrily challenging them to be angry back.

'What are you sorry about?' asked Cressida.

'For stealing your cakes.'

'Our cakes!' echoed the DDC in surprise.

'Yes. Don't you remember? When you were in Dragon's Wood rehearsing I came up to ask if I could join the DDC but Wolfgang here went and scoffed up all your goodies so I ran off with him instead.'

'But what are you doing here, hiding backstage?'

'I wanted to try again to ask if I could join your club so I came into the barn but no-one was here. Then I saw the brushes and the water and your outlines on the scenery which I thought were pretty rubbish and that I could do *much* better so I started doing a bit of painting then I got carried away and I was painting and painting and forgetting about everything else when suddenly I heard someone coming so I hid backstage. Wolfgang had got bored and gone off rabbiting then I heard him coming back and having a scrap with your collie and I knew he would find me and you would all be so cross.'

'Did you paint the borders round the posters at school as well?'

Alice nodded.

'The one with the woodcutter chasing a wolf chasing Rose?'

'And the one with the picnic basket with apples and sandwiches and chocolate cake and flapjacks?'

'And the one with the path and a stream and the Seven Dwarfs stepping stones?'

Alice nodded.

'I like it down at the Seven Dwarfs. You can go and paint down there in peace. And there is always clean

water. I take a jam jar and then I can just keep filling it from the stream. Got to keep your brushes clean when you're painting otherwise everything just comes out muddy.'

Sophie and Cressida felt themselves go red with embarrassment. To think they had mistaken Alice for a witch making lotions and potions.

'Did you paint round the cast list too?' asked Beaky tapping her nose.

'Yes, and what if I did?' asked Alice, defiantly.

'If you did you should join the DDC,' said Lou. 'We need a good artist and although I like painting I'm really busy with the costumes. What does everyone else think?'

'Yes!'

'Great idea!'

'Yes! We'd love you to join Alice!'

'Welcome aboard the DDC!'

'STOP!' shouted Sophie. The situation was getting out of her control. The Daisy Drama Club had been *her* idea and *Cressie's* idea and now everybody else seemed to be making important decisions like who was going to be in it! 'We can't just have people barging in, stealing our food, painting all over our posters and scenery and hiding backstage and then saying they want to join. So I say NO!'

'Leaping liquorice! I say YES!' said Harry.

'Leaping liquorice! I say YES too,' said Hen.

'YES!' 'YES!' 'YES!' 'YETH!'

It was a rebellion!

A revolution!

Sophie felt so angry tears pricked her eyes and to her horror she started sobbing.

'I say NO!' Still sobbing and gulping for breath she turned to Cressida. 'What about you Cress?'

Sophie and Cressida were very best friends and never argued but this was a very tricky situation.

Whose side would Cress take?

Everyone looked at Cress waiting ... wondering ..

But Cressida was too diplomatic just to take sides and replied quickly, 'As founders of the Daisy Drama Club Sophie and I will hold an emergency meeting right now in the Daisy Drama Club's HQ. Come on Sophie.'

Sophie, still trembling with anger, followed Cress across the yard and up to Sophie's bedroom.

'How could they just start deciding things like that? Under our very noses Cress. Lou saying people can join our club - people like angry Alice who we don't even know!'

Sophie started sobbing again, in fury.

Cressida chewed on the end of her pencil thinking.

'First,' she said thoughtfully, 'we've got to get back control so I hereby elect you as President of the Daisy Drama Club and you can elect me as the other President of the Daisy Drama Club.'

'Can you have *two* presidents?' asked Sophie through her sobs. 'Wouldn't one of us have to be vice-president.'

'Not if you are best friends like we are. Best friends are an unusual case and can both be presidents at the same time and that means we are both equally in charge.'

Cressida had an uncle who was pretty important in politics in America so she knew all about this sort of thing.

'And what do we do next?' asked Sophie.

'Well, now we've had the election we can have a

vote to see if we should let Alice join or not. Shut your eyes and put up your hand if you think YES, sit on your hand if you think NO. Open your eyes.'

Cressida's hand was up in the air.

Sophie was sitting on her hand.

'That's not a full YES or a full NO, so it means she can only join on a few weeks trial, which will include the performance of *Red Riding Hood*. Then the presidents, that's me and you, will have another vote. If we both vote YES she can join, and if we both vote NO she can't and if we have one YES and one NO Alice will have to stay on trial until we both agree.'

Sophie hugged Cressie. She had felt the DDC was slipping away from them and now it was firmly back as Sophie and Cressida's very own club!

Sophie and Cressida went back to the barn and explained that after elections, consultation, debate and a presidential vote, Alice could join on a trial basis.

'S'pose that's better than not joining at all,' said Alice, not sure if she was pleased or not.

'You'll just have to fill in a temporary membership application form,' said Cressie. 'First of all do you have any infectious diseases?'

Alice hadn't and managed to answer all the questions satisfactorily.

'That's it then. Welcome to the Daisy Drama Club Alice, for now at least.'

For the first time Alice smiled.

'Great!' she said grinning. 'You won't regret it!'

Everyone felt like clapping, so they did.

'Hey, I don't suppose there is a part going is there?' said Alice forgetting to be angry and defiant.

'Yes there is!' said Lou. 'I've got two parts - Mother and Mist. You can be Mist if you like. I'm finding it very confusing trying to do both!'

'Wait Lou!' cut in Sophie feeling angry again. 'You can't decide the casting just like that! Cressie and I are in charge of casting. What do you think Cressida?'

Cressida put her hand up and Sophie did too.

'Right! That's *properly* decided,' said Sophie 'Lou will be Mother and Alice, you can take the part of Mist.'

'Good stuff!' said Alice delighted.

'It just goes to show,' said Lou, 'writing in an extra part is never a bad thing! Well done Beaky!'

But the words *'an extra part is never a bad thing'* whirled around in Beaky's mind. As it turned out it *was* a good thing. Which reminded Beaky about the other little problem.

'While we are talking about parts, I just have a little suggestion for the Trees of the Wood chorus,' she said tentatively.

'Yes?' said everyone.

'I love doing Trees of the Wood!' said Abby interrupting. 'It's really fun. You'll love it Alice.'

'Ah,' said Beaky. 'You see the thing is ... I was thinking about the Trees of the Wood ...'

Everyone looked at Beaky.

'And?' asked Cressida.

Beaky just went bright red.

'While Beaky is just thinking what she was thinking about the Trees of the Wood I've been thinking about the costumes,' interrupted Lou. 'Most of your drawings were really helpful - some more than others …'

Lou showed everyone the costume book she had put together and paused on Abby's design for her Shimmermist costume.

It was Abby's turn to go bright red.

Shimmermist

'Great costumes,' said Lou, ' can only be created if the starting point is great design, and that, Abby,' she added pointing at Abby's drawing, 'is doomed to failure.'

'It is terrible!' admitted Abby. 'I just *couldn't* draw a Shimmermist costume.'

'Looks like a bin liner with a swimming hat on top,' said Alice scornfully. 'Terrible. I'll have another go for you Abby. I can imagine it already.'

Abby looked greatly relieved. It had been bad enough trying to draw the costume. Just think how embarrassing it would have been if Lou had made it into a costume and she had had to go on stage wearing what, now she looked at it again, did look very much like a bin liner with a swimming hat stuck on top. Thank goodness for Alice!

The rehearsal finished and Beaky had failed to tell the cast about the Monday Club. The problem for Beaky was not getting smaller but getting bigger and bigger and more serious and complicated. If Sophie and Cressida found out she had not only cast one extra person in the play without telling them they would be cross. But there were *five* new members of the cast that the directors knew nothing about.

Poor Beaky could not help thinking that a disaster of gigantic proportions was looming!

A Woodcutter's Tale

As an ex-Bavarian woodcutter, Uncle Max was invited to The Barn Theatre to give Harry some tuition on how to be a convincing woodcutter.

'Put your axe over your shoulder like this and whistle. Just like milkmen, all woodcutters whistle. Now when it comes to chopping, swing your axe in time to your whistling. The main thing is to jump out of the way when the tree comes down. Splendid Harry! Being a woodcutter is the finest most noble profession in the world and you are a natural!'

'Why did you *stop* being a woodcutter Uncle Max?' asked Harry. Everyone called Uncle Max 'Uncle Max' even though he was really only Sophie's uncle. Uncle Max's glasses started to steam up and his voice went a bit funny and he was just about to run outside when he suddenly changed his mind and, taking a deep, deep, deep breath, said, 'I'll tell you if you're all sitting comfortably ...'

And this is the incredible tale
Uncle Max told
the Daisy Drama Club ...

The Story of Max the Woodcutter.

Once upon a time there was a woodcutter chopping down trees in a great forest in deepest, darkest Bavaria. He was a strong, fine young man, very handsome and he was whistling whilst he worked.

Suddenly he heard a terrifying howl.

'Hooooowwww!'

So he stopped and there slinking it's way through the trees was an enormous wolf. The wolf was hungry and leapt at the woodcutter but the woodcutter was brave and bold and slashed back at it with his axe. The wolf howled again.

'Hooooowwww!'

and slunk off into the forest.

Seconds later the brave and bold woodcutter heard a scream.

'Aaaaaaaaaah! Help! Help!'

Someone was in trouble!

The woodcutter ran through the trees and saw the wolf about to pounce on a young lady who was carrying a basket of goodies so the woodcutter leapt at the wolf and this time slew him in one stroke!

The young lady was very grateful and offered him some chocolate cake from her basket of goodies. The woodcutter accepted gratefully and they sat down on the grass together which was a little damp so the woodcutter quickly skinned the wolf and made a nice rug for the young lady.

'Were you on your way to your grandmother's house with that basket of goodies? asked the woodcutter.

'No. Why would I be? I do not have a grandmother. I am all alone in the world. My job is delivering cake to woodcutters. replied the young lady.

The woodcutter and the young lady chatted a little longer. She was very beautiful and he was very handsome so naturally they fell in love and decided to get married.

The day before the wedding the woodcutter was out chopping trees when tragedy struck. One of the trees fell on him and pinned him to the ground. He could not move. As hard as he tried he could not lift the branch and was stuck there for seven days.

On the seventh day he was so weak he thought he would die. A great storm raged in the sky and a bolt of lighting crashed down and smote the branch pining him to the forest floor in two. He was free.

He leapt to his feet and ran to the church where he was to be married but when he got there it was empty. A little note was left on the altar. It said,

'I waited for seven days but you did not come. My heart is broken and I have run out into the storm and will wonder the world looking for you. xxxxxxxxxxxxxxxxxxxxxxxxxxxxxxxxxxxxxxxxxxx

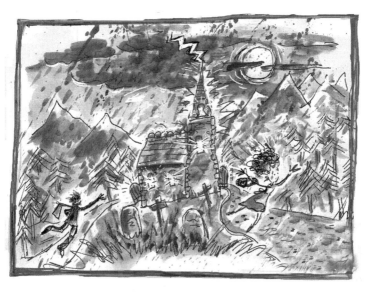

The woodcutter ran out of the church into the storm but there was no sign of the young lady. So the woodcutter too wandered the world but he never found her.

And that is the end of the story.

'What happened in the end end?' asked Harry.

The woodcutter gave up chopping wood and joined the theatre where he made wooden frames. But he never gave up hope of finding the young lady, and he never will. Perhaps she is still looking too.

With that Uncle Max gave a gulp and a big sigh and his glasses steamed up and a great tear dropped off the end of his beard. He blew his nose in his large spotty handkerchief.

'Uncle Max, ith that woodcutter you?' asked Susie bravely.

Uncle Max nodded into his handkerchief.

'What did the lady look like?'

'She was very beautiful. Lovely long blond curly hair, blue eyes, pink cherry lips but the most wonderful thing of all was her smile. It was as bright a smile as the summer sunshine and when she smiled she got little dimples in her cheeks. How I loved those dimples!'

'It thoundth like a fairy thtory to me,' said Susie, 'and all fairy stories end happily ever after tho I'm thore you will find the beautiful lady one day.'

'You're right Susie!' said Uncle Max with a gulp. 'I'll never give up! Never!'

And with that Uncle Max jumped into his old banger and drove out of the yard.

The Daisy Drama Club all stayed very quiet thinking about poor Uncle Max.

'I think we should do thomething to help your Uncle Max Thophie.'

'So do I! I had no idea that he had such a story to tell.'

'Perhaps we should put up some posters?'

'What - just in Wissop? I can't see *that* would do any good?'

'But you never know,' said Susie. 'One thing might lead to another.'

'I'll do them if you like,' volunteered Alice. 'From Uncle Max's description I reckon I know exactly what the beautiful lady would look like.'

Alice was as good as her word and soon a 'LOST Woodcutter's lovely-missing-wife-to-be' poster was pinned up on the Wissop village noticeboard.

It seemed very unlikely that any good would come of it but at least it was something and *something* was always better than *nothing*.

On Guard!

Now Harry knew how to act like a woodcutter but she and Hen were having problems with their stage fight ...

Sometimes they giggled.

Sometimes they got cross.

Sometimes they ended up arguing.

Sometimes they ended up fighting - but not *stage* fighting - just fighting each other.

The problem was they could never remember their moves and did not know *how* to move to make the fighting look in the least bit convincing.

The scene went like this:

```
WOODCUTTER Wolfee! We meet again but not for long!
   Take that! And that!

Woodcutter uses his axe to chop at Wolfee's feet.
Wolfee jumps over the axe as it hits the ground.

WOODCUTTER This axe is no good!
   If only I could afford a sword.

MIST hands WOODCUTTER a sword and takes his axe.

WOODCUTTER Good Lord! A sword!

SHIMMERMIST Wait! I think we should make it fair
   For Wolfee too!
   So here's a sword for you!
```

99

(hands Wolfee a sword)
Be prepared!
Arms by your side! Under your chin!
Let the duel begin!

WOODCUTTER and WOLFEE On guard!

Woodcutter and Wolfee have a sword fight. Clashing of swords, leap over furniture, Woodcutter is nearly lost, he pushes off Wolfee, Wolfee is dramatically killed. Wolfee lies on the ground motionless.

Grandpa Albert came to watch Harry and Hen rehearse. The fight was not impressive.

'What Harry and Hen need is a super dooper combat expert who can show them how to do proper stage fighting,' sighed Beaky.

'I think I might know the very person to help Harry and Hen,' said Albert tapping his nose.

Beaky sighed. This sounded like trouble!

'Harry and Hen,' said Albert. 'I am going to take you for a lesson with an expert in combat who might be able to give you a few stage fight tips. But I am going to have to sneak you into the building as visitors are forbidden so you've got to be as quiet as mice.'

'Oh! That thoundth exciting,' said Susie. 'Could I come too. It would be good training for when I am a forenthic detective. I will alwayth be going on thecret mithons, thneaking into buildingth and I might need to learn how to fight and defend mythelf.'

Only Cress really understood what Susie meant, but one thing was for sure, nobody wanted to miss out on this adventure. Instead of just Harry and Hen, Albert found *all* the DDC piling into Miranda.

It wasn't a long journey and Beaky was pretty sure she knew where they were going - Battleaxe Barracks! How on earth would she keep the Trees of the Wood secret secret now!

'Here we are,' said Albert parking Miranda in a back lane. 'Quiet as mice and follow me!'

Albert led the way to a large Victorian house. Instead of going down the front garden path he hopped over the garden fence and dived into a large rhododendron bush, the DDC in tow.

'Keep down and keep quiet!' he ordered.

In the bush was a string tied to a branch. The string ran out of the bush, across the front garden and up to a little hole drilled into the brick of the house on the first floor.

Albert pulled the string sharply three and a half times. Far, far away Abby, who had very good hearing thought she could hear a ringing sound.

'Why is the doorbell in this bush?' she asked Albert.

'Shhh!' came the reply. 'Just watch.'

Seconds later a sash window on the ground floor shot up and a figure whistled three and a half times then disappeared.

'That's the all clear!' whispered Albert in a very loud whisper so that he could hear it too. 'Hurry!'

Albert sprinted across the front lawn, jumping privet hedges and rose bushes and swung his long legs over the ledge of the wide open sash window and landed in the house. The DDC followed, tumbling over one another as they climbed in.

'Tiptoes only,' said Albert in a whisper so loud that it made Cressida go 'Shhh!'

Albert led them up a great wide oak staircase, onto a great wide oak landing and along to a great wide oak door. He knocked on the great wide oak door three and a half times. Immediately a voice said,

'Identify yourself stranger!'

'Did you hear anything?' Albert whispered to the DDC, in a shouty way.

'Someone said 'Identify yourself stranger',' said Beaky as loudly as she dared.

'Agent Hopscotch!' shouted Albert in a loud quiet voice.

'Enter,' came the reply.

'Did you hear anything?' Albert whispered to the DDC, in a shouty way.

'Someone said 'Enter',' said Beaky as loudly as she dared.

Albert turned the great wide oak handle of the great wide oak door very, very slowly and very, very slowly opened the great wide oak door and led the way into a great wide oak room.

'Is it safe?' Albert whispered in a general direction, in a shouty way.

'Perfectly safe for forty three and three quarter minutes,' came the reply.

The DDC were surprised to find themselves in a very pleasant sitting room. It was light and sunny and on sofas and chairs sat five old people, some knitting, some reading, some chatting and one playing chess.

The five old people looked up and stared at the DDC and the DDC stared at the five old people. Beaky felt herself going red.

After a while Cressie, because she thought it was about time *someone* said *something*, said, 'Good afternoon.'

A man whose face looked like a walnut said loudly, 'Right ho, who is ready for battle!' and he started whirling a lampstand around his head.

'Let me introduce Sir Hugh Digpot,' said Albert to the startled DDC. 'Sir Hugh is a distinguished expert in armed combat and will be able to teach you all you need to know to stage a convincing fight.'

Sir Hugh went straight into action.

'Right ho chaps! Who is playing Will the Woodcutter and who is playing Wolfee? *Red Riding Hood's* classic *Man-Versus-Beast* scene isn't it?'

The DDC were amazed. How did Sir Hugh know they were doing *Red Riding Hood*?

Beaky turned beetroot.

'I'm Will the Woodcutter,' said Harry.

'And I'm Wolfee,' said Hen.

'So we fight each other,' said Harry.

'We also use swords,' added Hen.

'Ah yes. *Man-Versus-Beast-With-Swords*,' said Sir Hugh thoughtfully. 'Stage fighting as you know is all about *illusion*. Slap, punch, kick, throw and hold! Attack and defend! All an illusion! An illusion! It has to be. Both protagonists need to survive for the next performance. If they don't the play itself becomes a dead duck! I'll demonstrate. Jim would you mind assisting?'

A hat who was playing chess against himself looked up. 'Pleased to oblige Sir Hugh. Not sure what to do with that pesky bishop. A little exercise might clear the mind.'

Jim the Hat stood up and flexed his muscles.

'Ready and willing, Sir Hugh!'

Sir Hugh and Jim went into action; they leapt about the sitting room in the most fearsome, fantastic death-defying display, dive bombing over sofas, swinging chairs at each other, hanging from the curtains and swordfighting with lampstands.

'Get the drift?' squeaked Sir Hugh as he was held upside down by Jim who was swinging from the chandelier.

Harry and Hen nodded, impressed.

The rest of the elderly people clapped.

'Jolly good! Jolly good!' said a sharp old lady snappily.

Sophie nudged Cress. 'Look,' she whispered. 'It's ancient Miss Windrush.'

'Your go chaps!' said Sir Hugh to Harry and Hen. 'Let me down Jim.'

Jim let Sir Hugh go and the octogenarian plus tumbled onto a Persian rug in an impressive controlled fall.

'Now your go girls.'

There followed ten minutes of violent grappling during which time Sir Hugh taught Harry and Hen an impressive routine.

'Now for the swordfight. Rapiers, smallswords or broadswords? Take your pick.'

Sir Hugh held out a rolled up newspaper, a fire poker and a lampstand.

Harry took the newspaper and Hen took the lampstand. Sir Hugh taught them to attack and defend shouting out instructions ...

'... never get close enough to hit each other with your weapon! ...'

'... block! ...'

'... lunge! ...'

'... lunge! ...'

'... block! ...'

'... thrust! ...'

'... block! ...'

'... somersault! ...'

'... block! ...'

'... somersault! ...'

'... dive! ...'

'... flip over! ...'

'... swing from the chandelier ...'

'... Hen cartwheel onto Harry's shoulders ...'

'... Harry leapfrog over Hen and up onto the mantlepiece ...'

'... climb up the curtains and swing - 2 - 3 - 4! Try to get a rhythm into it! Swing - 2 - 3 - 4 ...'

'... role Harry up in the Persian rug and whirl her round the room - 4 - 5 - 6 ...'

'... leap onto the high backed chair Hen and let it tip back - no don't worry about Miss Windrush - she will enjoy the ride - now jump off - yes! Lovely dismount ...'

'... grab an old person and give them a jolly good whirl round before letting go - that's it, just like a shot put - super Harry ...'

'... now you always need a fantastic, fabulous, knock out sensational finale. Harry grab that portrait of King Charles I hanging over the mantelpiece and smash it down over Hen's head ...'

Harry hesitated.

'Don't worry about the painting dear, I did it,' said the wispy lady with the breathy voice. 'I can always paint another one. Go on. Have a good smash-bang-wallop!'

Harry pulled the painting off the wall and with more enjoyment than she felt she ought to have felt brought the painting down on her sister's head.

Hen fell to the ground as if she were dead!

Everyone applauded.

'That is a brilliant way to finish the fight!' said Cressida.

'I could do a painting for our play,' said Alice 'so

Will the Woodcutter could knock out Wolfee on stage in just the same way.'

'Do you paint dear?' asked the wispy old lady. 'Such a lovely pastime!'

'Oh yes,' said Alice. 'I paint all the time. I've just done a poster of a beautiful lady that I've never seen. It's for a woodcutter. He wanted to marry her but lost her. All I know is that she has long blond hair, blue eyes, cherry lips, a sunshiny smile and dimples when she smiles.'

'*Dimples* did you say?' said the sharp lady sharply, who had been eavesdropping on their conversation.

'Yes. Dimples.'

The word flew round the room like wildfire, passed on from one old person to the next.

'Where is the poster?' snapped the sharp lady.

'On the noticeboard in the village.'

'Noticeboard!' snapped the sharp old lady. 'Something must be done!'

But Alice wasn't listening. She was enjoying talking to the wispy lady about painting. 'I'd like to have a go at more portraiture but right now I mainly paint scenery. We've only just moved into the village and I like painting all the trees and woods. They almost have as much character as people I reckon.'

'Absolutely!' agreed the wispy old lady. 'Reminds

me of a little tune we have been practising. But I suppose you know all about that.'

'I don't think I do,' said Alice.

'Oh dear! Must be some muddle and confusion. Everything is always muddle and confusion.'

'Would you like to hear it?' snapped the sharp lady who was still eavesdropping on their conversation.

'That would be lovely,' said Alice feeling a bit muddled and confused herself.

Beaky screeched in horror and dived behind the curtains. She had no doubt *whatsoever* what was coming next!

'We've got actions too,' snapped the sharp lady. 'Help me out of my chair.'

Alice helped the sharp lady stand up, noticing how paper thin her skin was and how you could see the blue veins running beneath like little streams. Once standing the old lady clapped her hands together snappily, like a bird flapping its wings.

All the old people wearily heaved themselves up and out of their chairs and huffing and puffing lined up. The sharp lady counted 'One, two three!', then snapped her stick like fingers together so they made a sudden explosion, like a fire cracker going off.

The effect was tremendous.

The old people started ...

    to sing ...

        to chant ...

            to rock and roll ...

```
We are the Trees of the Wood,
Some are bad and some are good!
We are the Trees of the Wood,
Some are bad and some are good!
```

```
(WISPY VOICE) I'm very beautiful.
(SIR HUGH) I'm very strong.
(MISS WINDRUSH) I'm very l ... l ... long!
(JIM THE HAT) I'm very bendy.
(NO VOICE) I can sing a song ... La!
```

```
We are the Trees of the Wood,
Some are bad and some are good!
We are the Trees of the Wood,
Some are bad and some are good!
```

```
(MISS WINDRUSH) I'm very, very tall.
(JIM THE HAT)And I'm the smallest of them all.
(NO VOICE) If you climb me you might fall ...
(SIR HUGH) I ah ... ah ... ah.. SNEEZE
(WISPY VOICE) And I have trouble with
     ... buzzzzz ... bees!
```

```
We are the Trees of the Wood,
Some are bad and some are good!
We are the Trees of the Wood,
Some are bad and some are good! YEAH!
```

The DDC could not believe their eyes or their ears.

'We've been practising!' said Sir Hugh proudly. 'What do you think Beaky? Beaky, where are you?'

'Splendid! Marvellous! Fantasticalicas!' came a mumbling from behind the curtains.

'Beaky,' said Sophie and Cressida, 'what *is* going on?'

'We're going to be in your play,' said Sir Hugh to Sophie and Cressida. 'Did you forget to tell them Beaky dear?' he called to the curtain.

Before Beaky could answer a door slammed downstairs.

In an instant the old people froze. The atmosphere changed from excitement to fear.

'She's back,' said the wispy lady in her breathy voice.

'Posts!' snapped Miss Windrush, grabbing some knitting she had tucked down the side of her upright armchair.

'Quick! This way!' said Sir Hugh to the DDC and opened a door in the bookshelf that looked like a bookshelf but was in fact a door.

'Albert,' said Sir Hugh, speaking with great urgency, 'just get them safely out.'

Footsteps could be heard coming up the stairs.

'Who ith it?' asked Susie terrified.

'Our matron, Miss Gristlegrundelblug,' said the lady with the wispy voice, her eyes so big and full of fear that Susie did not have to ask, or want to ask what Miss Gristlegrundelblug was like.

With the rest of the DDC, Susie dashed through the bookshelf door and at top speed, followed Albert down the backstairs, out of the back door, down the back path through the back garden, out of the back gate, with a back entrance sign saying Battleaxe Barracks (Back Entrance) and into the back lane, called Back Lane, where Albert had parked Miranda. The DDC tumbled in and within seconds they were driving off and back to The Barn Theatre.

As soon as everyone was safely in Miranda questions rained down on Beaky.

'Beaky! What did they mean?'

'They are going to be in *our* play?'

'Why didn't you tell us?'

'How *could* you Beaky?'

'Beaky,' said Sophie, furious, 'you simply *can't* just ask people into our play. Cressida and I will not allow it. You'll have to go back and tell them no! No! No! NO!'

Beaky was as white as a sheet.

'Wait!' said Albert from the front. 'Don't blame Beaky. It's all my fault. Those old people, they are my dear friends. When they came to my house for their Monday Club as usual they were all very miserable with nothing to do except stare into the abyss of nothingness ... until they saw the *Red Riding Hood* script which I had left lying on the kitchen table. Despite being so stuffed with gloom and doom they were still naturally nosey so they picked up the script and started reading it and the next thing I knew was that they were chanting the *Trees of the Wood* song and deciding amongst themselves that they were jolly good at it and were going to be in your play and well they were old people transformed! Ping! It seemed a light had gone on! Suddenly they had a purpose in life. So I couldn't say NO and poor Beaky couldn't say NO either.'

'I don't think *we* can thay *NO* either,' said a small voice. It was Susie from somewhere on the back seat. 'I jutht can't help feeling tho thorry for them all shut up in that houth all tho frightened of Mith Grithelgrundel glug-glug-glug.'

'Have you ever seen Miss Gristlewhatshername Grandpa Albert? Is she very terrifying?'

Albert confessed he had never actually *seen* Miss Gristlegrundelblug but he had *heard* alot about her from the Monday Club - her horrible hairy legs as thick as tree trunks, her murky glasses with glass so murky you can't see where she is looking, her massive curly hair where she keeps a pet lizard, her voice so deep that it rumbles like a volcano, her ears so enormous she can hear your most secret thoughts, her cooking pot so black and grimy that everything tastes black and grimy, her heavy knit purple cardigan that moults little bits of wool everywhere so you can never really get away from her - sometimes the bits float in the air so you find yourself breathing her in which makes you nearly choke to death, - her singing voice that cracks the window pains and pops your ear drums, the way she hides in cupboards so when you go to get a broom she makes you jump out of your skin, the way she slides down the bannisters so that she can grab the newspaper first in the morning, the way she never folds the cereal packet over properly so that the cereal is always stale, the way she steams open all your letters and crosses out the nice bits or adds nasty bits so letters read like this - 'I do not hope you had a lovely holiday' or 'I do hope the weather was horrible', the way she ...'

At this point Miranda arrived at The Barn Theatre which was lucky as all the girls were sniffing and snuffling as they felt so sad for the residents of Battleaxe Barracks and the front window was so steamed up that Albert could hardly see out.

'Time for a vote,' whispered Cressida to Sophie. 'Hands up for YES, sit on your hand for NO.'

When Cressida opened her eyes both she and Sophie had raised their hands in the air.

'Sophie and I vote that we *should* let the Monday Club be in our play,' said Cressida to Albert.

'I know now why it would have been impothible for you to thay no Beaky,' said Susie.

Beaky and Albert looked greatly relieved.

'But how are they going to get to the performance if they are not allowed out?' asked Lou suddenly.

'Sir Hugh has a plan,' said Beaky, so happy that the DDC were no longer angry with her. 'It's called Operation Treefall. He's got maps and timetables and ropes and torches and flashing lights and compasses and penknives and invisible ink and a homing pigeon and sturdy boots.'

'That'th good then,' said Susie, reassured. 'Nothing can go wrong!'

Trespassers!

Only one week to go until The Performance!

After the sensational success of their first play the Daisy Drama Club had got a tiptop reputation. Tickets for *Red Riding Hood* soon became like gold dust in Wissop. Villagers were desperately buying tickets, reserving tickets and trying to get hold of them by means fair or foul. When it was rumoured that there were only a few tickets left a mini riot broke out in Gumtree Stores and Mr Gumtree himself had to break up the rioters by means of wielding a large leek. This was super exciting as last time it had been tricky for Sophie and Cressida to sell *any* tickets at all!

'Just shows, you can really build on the success of your last performance,' said Cressie as she sat cross legged on Sophie's bed making a list of the audience. 'We've sold forty-six tickets and The Barn Theatre only properly seats forty! We'll have to ask your dad if we can put those extra benches out.'

'And shall we have a lucky dip again like last time?'

'What about refreshments?'

'We could sell goodies in baskets, the same as Rose takes to her Grandmama.'

'Let's ask everyone to ask their mums to make

flapjacks and fairy cakes and get some red and white check napkins to wrap them in.'

Cressida wrote everything down on her *Things To Do List (12)*.

'I can't believe it's already the dress rehearsal this week. Our last rehearsal before the actual play!'

'I wish the Trees of the Wood could be here. How can we rehearse properly if half the cast are missing?'

How could Sophie and Cressida, as Yellow Feathers and Flapper, perfect their flying-in-and-out-of-trees-routine if the trees were not there?

How could Wolfee chase Rose through a non-existant wood?

How could Will the Woodcutter chop down trees in a forest made of fresh air?

'We are all meant to be actors so I suppose we ought to be able to *pretend* that the Trees of the Wood are on stage,' said Cressida.

'But Cressie, that would be fine if they were *not* going to be there on the night,' said Sophie, 'but if they *are* we need to rehearse their entrances and exits and their positions on stage otherwise we are going to keep on crashing into each other and it's going to be one big chaotic calamity!'

'You're right Sophie,' said Cressie. 'We need to do something before it's too late.'

'We need them to come to the dress rehearsal.'

The girls sat in silence - but only for a split second.

Sophie and Cressida looked at each other knowing what each other was thinking as only best friends do.

'Let's invite them!' they said together.

Cressida wrote a note and they set off down to Battleaxe Barracks passing the noticeboard where Alice had pinned up the 'LOST. Woodcutter's Lovely-Missing-Wife-To-Be' poster.

'I do hope we find Uncle Max's beautiful lady,' sighed Sophie staring at Alice's portrait of the lovely-missing-wife-to-be. 'He seems so happy that we are trying to help him that I just don't want to disappoint him. But she could be anywhere in the world.'

'Anywhere!' added Cressida.

They did not notice that a sharp old lady, who had been heading for the noticeboard, had seen the girls coming and gasped and turned instead to pick berries from a bush on the other side of the road.

They did not notice that as soon as they walked on the sharp old lady doddered at top speed over to the noticeboard and got out a large black pen and drew a thick bushy moustache and big bushy eyebrows over the lovely-missing-wife-to-be's face. Then she ran off down the road at top doddery pace, chuckling to herself. 'Hee! Hee! Hee!'

Meanwhile Sophie and Cressida had walked on in silence both trying to think how the beautiful lady had vanished into thin air.

'I hope we don't bump into Miss Gristlegrundelblug,' said Cressida as they neared Battleaxe Barracks. 'She might force us to tell us what we are doing and then the old people will never be allowed out to perform.'

For a second Sophie thought this might not be such a bad thing. Perhaps Miss Gristlegrundelblug could turn from enemy to ally and help them by locking the old people in. But that would be too mean for words!

❀ 121 ❀

'Let's not take any risks,' whispered Sophie as they reached Battleaxe Barracks. So instead of going up to the front door and ringing the front door bell, the girls slipped into the garden and hid in the rhododendron bush. They watched the house for a few minutes to see if Miss Gristlegrundelblug was about. Nothing.

Then they heard footsteps.

Sophie and Cressida froze in fear.

Was it Miss Gristlegrundelblug?

They breathed a sigh of relief when they recognised the ancient figure of Miss Windrush, who rushed down the front path at top doddering pace with a basket of berries, and disappeared in through the front door.

'She must be so brave escaping to forage for food like that,' whispered Cressida in admiration.

The girls waited again to make sure Miss Gristlegrundelblug was nowhere to be seen.

All clear!

Sophie pulled on the piece of string which was still tied to a branch. Far away they could hear a bell ringing. Seconds later the downstairs sash window flew open with a bang crash and Sir Hugh shoved his head out.

'Who's there?' he shouted aggressively.

Sophie and Cressida dashed across the grass, leaping over the privet hedge and roses.

'We've come to give you this!' whispered Cressida thrusting the invitation into his hand.

'Who on earth are you? If you've come to invade you better buzz off! Go on! Buzz off!'

And then to the girls horror Sir Hugh poked a broom handle through the open window and started firing shots into the air and yelling at the top of his voice, 'Trespassers! Bang! Bang! Trespassers! Bang! Bang!'

All the windows upstairs shot open and four old people leaned out, and started firing with lampstands and pokers and rolled up newspapers and yelling at the tops of their voices, 'Trespassers! Bang! Bang! Trespassers! Bang! Bang!'

Sophie and Cressida did not wait for any explanation. Any second now the terrifying Miss Gristlegrundelblug would burst out of the front door and capture them. Already they could hear heavy footsteps crashing down the stairs!

'Quick Cressie!' yelled Sophie. 'Run!'

OPERATION TREEFALL : Section A

The dress rehearsal started badly.

Alice had designed sensational floaty, flipsy, wispy, watery outfits for Shimmermist and Mist and Lou had stayed up until midnight sewing, stitching and snipping so that all the costumes would be ready - but then disaster struck!

At least half of the costumes didn't fit.

Hen tore her Wolfee outfit trying to get into the furry top.

'Hen, you fatso!' cried Lou in dismay. 'You are much fatter than when I measured you for your costume!'

Susie's cloak was so long it trailed along on the ground and she kept tripping up.

'Susie! You have *definitely* shrunk since I measured you!'

Sophie and Cressida tried on their Yellow Feathers and Flapper outfits. One was yellow, Yellow Feathers, and one was white, Flapper. Lou had made magnificent wings for both of them using some very large feathers which she had bought from a specialist sewing shop. Sophie and Cressida were thrilled. It was amazing how much more bird like they felt when they actually had feathers.

Lou looked a little happier until one of Cressie's feathers fell out and by the time Harry's woodcutter waistcoat split Lou was in tears. She was exhausted from her midnight sewing marathon trying to get everything just perfect for today and now it seemed all her efforts were wasted.

'Don't worry Lou!' said Harry brightly. 'Me and Hen are pretty good at sewing! We'll help you finish off.'

Hen looked surprised. She and Harry were terrible at sewing.

Harry proceeded to sew the wolf's tail onto the woodcutters jacket and Hen cut a big hole in Rose's cloak by mistake.

'Oh this is ghastly! Quite ghastly!' cried Lou. 'Why did I ever, ever say I would do the costumes?'

Meanwhile Shimmermist's costume still hung on the rail. Abby had not even turned up.

'She's forgotten the dress rehearsal,' muttered Sophie. 'Unforgiveable!'

'Let's get started,' said Cressida feeling tensions rising.

Once the rehearsal started things went from bad to worse. Beaky, as prompt, was finding it hard to know when to prompt and when to wait.

```
    A chap like me ...
```
she whispered to Hen.

'I know! I know!' came back the reply from Hen. 'I was just acting!'

And Hen said her following lines with gusto to prove the point.

```
Look here Rose, we all need our fuel,
And I need something more solid than gruel,
A chap like me needs something to really crunch.
I like gristle and bone for my lunch.
Something to grind and chew ...
Something just like YOU!
```

After that it went from worse to cataclysmically worse.

Susie was being chased by Wolfee through the wood.

'Thall I pretend the trees are on the thtage or not, Thophie? Could we put some chairs where they might be? It'th tho difficult not knowing exactly where they will be thtanding ... or will they be juth growing?'

Sophie and Cressie put chairs on stage but in the dashing about the chairs kept getting knocked over.

'Thith is hopeleth! I'm thore profethional actorth do not have to wait until opening night to get all the catht together!'

Backstage under the prompt light Beaky went red. She still felt a bit guilty.

Sophie and Cressida were worried. Everything was a disaster - the costumes were chaos, their invitation to the Trees of the Wood had been a calamity, the performance was all stop and start, stop and start and where was Abby?

Suddenly they heard a hurried clip clop, clip clop.

Seconds later, just as Harry and Hen were in mid-fight, Abby burst into the barn.

'I'm so, so, so sorry!' she said. 'I set off *ages* ago but Pickle was being so naughty! There was a new little copse of trees that seemed to have sprung up overnight and Pickle would *not* go past them! He was completely spooked! He kept whirling round and round and round and being very silly indeed. Anyway I'm here now and ready to do my Shimmermisting.'

'That's no excuse!' said Sophie angrily. Not many directors would have to put up with such outrageously ridiculously unreliable behaviour!

'Poor Pickle,' said Cressida, trying to smooth the waters. 'Look Abby, Lou has made you a wonderfully shimmery misty costume so why don't you see if it fits and let's get on with the rehearsal.'

During their break Sophie's mum brought the now traditional basket of goodies into The Barn Theatre.

'Odd,' she said as she put the basket down. 'As I was coming back from Gumtree Stores just now, I saw a little copse of trees along Blacksmith Lane that I am *sure* was not there before.'

She went out looking puzzled.

Just then Uncle Max drove into the barn in his old banger.

'Good morning Daisies! I just thought I would come in and see how the dress rehearsal is going - but oh my! Oh my! I have seen a miracle! A vision!'

'Your beautiful lady?' cried Susie her eyes wide in excitement.

'Have you found her?'

 128

'Where is she?'

'Did she recognise you?'

'No! Not that ... but something very odd *has* just happened! I have just seen five trees on the grassy verge. Nothing strange about that but as I was driving along they seemed to be moving too. As soon as I stopped the car they stopped and when I drove on and looked in my mirror they were running along. They were chasing me! I'm going mad! I must be!'

Beaky started tapping her nose anxiously.

Suspicious goings on!

Then she gasped.

A leafy, branchy arm had wound its way round the barn door. Within seconds a whole forest was crowding into The Barn Theatre.

'Here at last!' said one of the trees. '*OPERATION TREEFALL : Section A* successfully completed. Trees of the Wood reporting for dress rehearsal duty as requested by directors Miss Sophie and Miss Cressida. Apologies for rudeness on calling you trespassers Miss Sophie and Miss Cressida when you were on your dangerous mission to deliver the dress rehearsal info but I was suspicious that you were enemy invaders. And you can never be too careful in these situations. Now we've got to be quick before Miss Gristlegrundelblug discovers we're missing. In fact! Oh heavens! It's taken us so long to get here I think we ought to scarper right now! Trees of the Wood! About turn!'

The trees were about to march straight out of the barn when Beaky went into action.

'Please don't go!' she said tapping her nose. 'You've risked so much to get this far that you must rehearse with us otherwise it will be a dangerous mission wasted. I'll run round to Grandpa's house and ask him to give you a lift back in Miranda.'

'I'll go,' said Uncle Max. 'Now I know I'm not going mad and really *was* being chased by trees I feel much better! You stay here and rehearse Beaky.'

Uncle Max rushed off, keen to escape from the trees and the dress rehearsal continued in earnest.

Dress Rehearsal

'I love the painting over the fireplace. Did you paint it dear?' a tree with a wispy voice asked Alice as they all waited backstage.

'Yes,' whispered back Alice. 'It was going to be Grandmama but I changed it to your Miss Gristlegrundelblug so that when Will the Woodcutter smashes it over Wolfee's head he can do it with real gusto. I've never seen Miss Gristle-grundelblug but do you think it looks like her?'

The wispy tree chuckled. 'Exactly as one would imagine her. Oh dearie me! Funny! Very funny!'

Meanwhile Lou, also squashed backstage with the trees was admiring their costumes and just had to find out more. 'Who made your costumes?' she asked the nearest branches.

'We just did our best from cutting up curtains and foraging for twigs and leaves in the garden,' said a sharp voice. 'Miss Gristlegrundelblug would never allow us to spend money buying material for trifles such as costumes!'

'Miss Windrush!' thought Sophie and Cressida.

'Then I just sewed everything together. Speediest seamstress one could wish to meet! Who made *your* costumes?'

'I did,' said Lou embarrassed. 'They're a disaster - all falling apart.'

'Nonsense!' snapped the sharp tree. 'You clearly have the vision! The ideas! The style! They look magnificent - just need a little strengthening in the seams which is the easy bit. I'll help you.'

'At last,' thought Lou. 'Someone who can actually sew!'

Within seconds Lou and her branchy friend had escaped from backstage and were hard at work finishing off the wardrobe, keeping a sharp eye on the rehearsal so they could down pins and needles and dash on stage when needed!

The dress rehearsal *with* the Trees of the Wood was so much better than the rehearsal *without* the Trees of the Wood, who were very pleased to see that their idea for birds in the cast was so successful.

'Again!' called the tree with the hat, after Cressie, Sophie, Hen and The Trees of the Wood had rehearsed Act 1 Scene 2:

```
YELLOW FEATHERS Eek!
    (frightened on spotting Wolfee) Hello Wolfee.

FLAPPER What are you up to?

YELLOW FEATHERS No good I bet.

WOLFEE (trying to be charming)
    Oh hello little duck and little bird.
    How absurd
    To suggest that I was up to no good.
    I was just thinking about my lunch.
    I mean, what a pretty bunch
    Of delicious, juicy, scrumptious ...
(looking at Flapper and licking his lips)
    ... er daisies those are.

FLAPPER We don't trust you Wolfee
    When you start licking your lips.

YELLOW FEATHERS You're thinking of food ...

FLAPPER ... and we don't mean chips!

WOLFEE Little duck! Little bird!
    You're so absurd.
    Be reasonable. Be fair.
    We all have to eat.
(Wolfee looks at Yellow Feathers and licks
 his lips)
    I say ducky!
    You have got a tasty looking pair of feet!
```

Wolfee makes a dash for Yellow Feathers

FLAPPER and YELLOW FEATHERS Screeeeech!

Yellow Feathers and Flapper fly around stage, in and out of Trees of the Wood, chased by Wolfee.

'It'th going to be a tiptop performanth!' said Susie speaking for the whole cast when they had finally reached the final finale.

'Till next Saturday!' said Sir Hugh.

'How will you get here without Miss Gristlegrundelblug finding out?' asked Cressida.

'That,' said Sir Hugh from within his costume, 'is *OPERATION TREEFALL : Section B*. It's a water-tight escape routine. Completely and utterly failsafe!'

Albert bundled the Trees of the Wood into Miranda, popped on his milkman's cap and, whistling, went off to deliver them back to Battleaxe Barracks before Miss Gristlegrundelblug found out they were missing.

OPERATION TREEFALL : Section 8

The day of The Performance ...

On the morning of the performance The Barn Theatre was bursting with activity.

Harry and Hen were ticking things off their *Prop List and Other Things* list.

Prop List and Other Things
- Woodland creatures sounds
    (pieces of paper on chairs for audience)
- Handkerchief
(for Granny to blow her nose on)
- Basket with Granny Cold Survival Kit
- Knife and fork
    (for Wolfee to eat Granny with)
- Axe (Will the Woodcutter)
- Sword 1 (Wolfee)
- Sword 2 (Will the Woodcutter)

Susie was helping Lou check that all the costumes were properly hung up on the rail that counted as the wardrobe. As well as wardrobe mistress, Lou was chief make-up artist so while she was still doing some final stitching she asked Susie to sort out the stage-make up box.

'What a meth!' cried Susie as she lifted the lid. A glitter pot had spilt and little glinting gold bits had erupted all over the brushes and sponges, the lid for long lash mascara had not been put on properly and there were black specs on the blusher box and some foundation cream had spurted all over the false hair.

'Thith is a dithgrath! My mother keeps her make-up box immaculate. I'll have to thort thith out!'

John was up on the first floor checking the lighting and trying not to be distracted by a little spider weaving a silky web.

Sophie and Cressida were putting out the chairs and extra benches.

Abby and Lou were organising the lucky dip and refreshment table.

All the tickets and many more were sold so Alice made a fierce sign saying *SOLD OUT* which they hung on the gate ...

... then they decided this looked a bit mean so they took it down again.

'I'm sure we can squeeze even more people in,' said Sophie, hating the idea of turning anyone away.

Everyone went home for lunch but nobody could eat a thing. 'My tummy is turning over and over and inside out and upside down with nerveth,' said Susie.

'You must eat,' insisted Mrs Theodora Whistle-White. 'A star cannot perform on an empty stomach. A plate of delicious spinach will give you the strength to razzle and dazzle on stage!'

'I can't! I'm thick with nerves and I'll be thick if I eat that thpinach,' wailed Susie. 'You eat it!'

'I can't. I'm sick with nerves too!' admitted Mrs Theodora Whistle-White.

They decided to abandon the spinach.

Everyone was back at Sophie's by five o'clock for make-up and to put on their costumes.

Lou had studied a wolf's face so she could make-up Hen to look as ferocious a beast as possible. She was making her own ...

Daisy Drama Club
Make-Up Instruction Manual

... and on page one she had written ...

HOW TO MAKE A FEROCIOUS WOLF

1. Cover face in white
2. Add grey and silver shadows

3. Draw a black line round the hair line
4. Paint nose black
5. Add squarish lines for the mouth
6. Use brush to create hairy lines around the face
7. Sweep black lines up from the outer corner of the eyes
8. Sweep black lines down from the inner corner of the eyes

Scarrry hairy!!!

Meanwhile down at Battleaxe Barracks the great escape, *OPERATION TREEFALL : Section B : part (i)* was going perfectly to plan.

All afternoon the inhabitants had pretended to feel ill so that Miss Gristlegrundelblug would not be suspicious if they all went to bed super early.

At 15.32 Jim the Hat started blowing his nose 15.32 extraordinarily loudly so that it would seem natural for him to pop off to bed early. He then went and put on his pyjamas, brushed his remaining few teeth and announced very loudly he was feeling so poorly that he was going to beddie-byes right now.

At 15.37 Miss Windrush sneezed snappily three 15.37 times and said that sounded a good idea and that she would do the same.

By 16.33pm all the elderly inhabitants of Battleaxe 16.33 Barracks were tucked up in bed snoring, sneezing, coughing and blowing their noses all struck down with terrible colds - or so it seemed ...

At 4.56pm Sir Hugh heard the front door 16.56 slamming downstairs and observed, in surprise, Miss Gristlegrundelblug hurrying out and up the front path. This was unexpected but Sir Hugh decided it was important to stick to *OPERATION TREEFALL : Section B : part (ii)* to the letter and not get diverted by unexpected diversions.

So in accordance with *OPERATION TREEFALL :*

Section B : part (ii) at 4.57pm Sir Hugh blew his whistle loudly one and half times. Everyone flung off their bed covers and rushed out of their bedrooms and onto the landing, coughing, sneezing and blowing their noses.

'We're in luck!' said Sir Hugh above the commotion. 'Miss Gristlegrundelblug has gone out.'

'Trust her to abandon ship when she thinks we are all dying in our beds!' muttered Jim the Hat, coughing and choking.

'She really should be looking after us in our weakened state,' added the wispy lady sneezing and spluttering breathily.

'You don't have to pretend you've got coughs and colds anymore!' said Sir Hugh. 'Miss Gristle-grundelblug has *gone out*!'

The sneezing, snuffling, coughing and spluttering stopped in an instant.

'Oh! I feel better already,' said the wispy lady.

'You can't feel better because you never were ill,' said the hat.

'No but *pretending* to be ill made me *feel* ill. Now I feel so much better!'

'That's because you are.'

'What?'

'Better.'

'But I never *was* ill.'

'No but you feel better *now* then when you weren't ill.'

Sir Hugh blew his whistle in irritation.

'Quick everyone - to your stations for *OPERATION* A FEW MINUTES LATER *TREEFALL : Section B : part (iii).'*

Everyone rushed back to their bedrooms, ripped the sheets off their beds, dashed back onto the landing and threw the great white cotton bundles into Sir Hugh's bedroom.

Then everyone rushed back to their own bedrooms again and stuffed jumpers and trousers and socks and underwear and coats and hats and walking sticks and teddy bears and photos and washbags and false teeth and eyepatches and false legs and wigs and spectacles and crossword puzzles and glass eyeballs and knitting and wheelchairs and crochet patterns and golf clubs and shotguns and bus passes and zimmer frames and sleeping pills and sketch books and binoculars down their beds and under their blankets and eiderdowns so that Miss Gristle-grundelblug would think they were still in bed and would never ever have the slightest weeniest idea that they were missing.

Then they all dashed into Sir Hugh's room for *OPERATION TREEFALL : Section B : part (iv).*

Sir Hugh had been busy and had tied his sheet to his bed. Tied to Sir Hugh's sheet was Jim the Hat's sheet. Tied to Jim's sheet was Miss Windrush's sheet. Tied to Miss Windrush's sheet was the wispy lady's sheet. Tied to the wispy lady's sheet was the voice that never spoke's sheet. Tied to the end of the voice that never spoke's sheet was the final knot.

'You first,' said Sir Hugh to Jim, as Sir Hugh threw the sheet rope out of the window.

Jim climbed onto the window ledge.

'Couldn't we go down the stairs?' asked Jim looking anxiously at the dark abyss below him.

'We are escaping from Miss Gristlegrundelblug,' retorted Sir Hugh.

'But she's gone out,' said Jim, 'so we don't really need to *escape*. We could just go down the stairs!'

'This is *OPERATION TREEFALL : Section B : part (iv),*' said Sir Hugh impatiently. 'Whatever the danger, whatever the sacrifice, we must follow the plan.'

'Besides, it's jolly good fun!' snapped Miss Windrush, who could not wait to have a go.

'Precisely. Off you go Jim!'

Jim the Hat climbed down the sheet rope. He got to the final knot and found himself dangling in mid-air.

'The rope is too short!'

142

Before Sir Hugh could answer Miss Windrush leaned out of the window and shouted down sharply, 'Don't be ridiculous man! The rope is not too short. YOU are too short. Just jump!'

The hat sighed and jumped.

'Aaaaaaah!'

'You all right down there?' called Sir Hugh.

'Perfectly all right,' called back the hat. 'The holly bush is just a bit prickly, that's all.'

'I'm next,' said Miss Windrush and she climbed out of the window.

'Wait!' came an urgent whisper from Jim.

'It's Miss Gristlegrundelblug! She's coming back!'

'But I'm half way down!' snapped Miss Windrush, holding on tightly.

'Just stay there, keep quiet and keep still!' said Jim. 'I'll distract her.'

Jim started coughing and choking and spluttering.

'Evening Miss Gristlegrundelblug! I just thought I would get a little fresh air before bed. Cough! Cough! Cough! Ooh I'm feeling so poorly! Could you help me back in through the front door. Yes I know, I'm sorry. I should never have come out. Very foolish! Silly me! Cough! Cough! Cough! Choke! Choke! Choke! Splutter! Splutter! Splutter!'

Jim walked off with Miss Gristlegrundelblug round to the front door, away from the holly bush and the dangling Miss Windrush.

With the danger of Miss Gristlegrundelblug past everyone climbed out. Eventually Sir Hugh was the last one left. He was just about to climb out of the window himself when there was a knock at his bedroom door. He froze. Miss Gristlegrundelblug!

Coughing and sneezing he went across and opened the door - and there stood Jim!

'What are *you* doing back up here!' spluttered Sir Hugh aghast.

'I had to come *in* with Miss Gristlegrundelblug so

I'll have to escape *out* again,' whispered Jim.

'Where is she now?'

'Oh I expect she's in her lounge on her pink fluffy sofa with her pink fluffy slippers on eating a box of chocolates. She had a big package under her arm when she came back.'

'Good. At least she's out of the way. But we still must hurry! We're getting short of time.'

Jim crossed over to the window and climbed down the rope for the second time, hastily followed by Sir Hugh.

Once the group had gathered on the lawn below they raced across, at top doddery speed, to the compost heap, behind which they had hidden their tree outfits.

'*OPERATION TREEFALL : Section B : part (v).* Tree costumes on!' commanded Sir Hugh. 'And remember, if we meet anybody on the way just stand absolutely still.'

QUITE A FEW MINUTES AFTER THAT

'Could we wave our arms around like branches waving in a gentle breeze - oooh! oooh! oooh! - to make us even more convincing as trees?' asked the wispy lady.

'Splendid idea!' said Sir Hugh. 'Everyone practise arm waving manoeuvre ... splendid ... now onwards to The Barn Theatre!'

The Show Must Go On!

Sophie was feeling horribly, sickeningly, desperately worried. She was backstage with the rest of the cast running through final ideas. The other side of the flats they could hear a happy buzz of anticipation from the audience. Even more benches had had to be put out and now The Barn Theatre audience was packed in like a tin of sardines. Mrs Theodora Whistle-White had arrived early to bag seats on the front row and was wearing her big furry coat. Lollipop had been snarling at the coat but Farmer Bagwash had asked Tim Stack, Cressida's dad who was so good with animals, to look after Lollipop, who had now settled down. The cast looked wonderful in their costumes and make-up and Sophie was confident that everyone knew their lines.

Nothing could go wrong ... except ...

... where were The Trees of the Wood?'

Not only was Sophie feeling so horribly, sickeningly, desperately worried - so was Cressida.

'I've just thought of something,' said Abby. 'Where are the Trees of the Wood?'

'They're on their way,' said Sophie trying to sound

confident. Whatever happened she and Cress could not let the rest of the cast know they were worried otherwise everyone might lose their nerve and that would be a disaster.

The whole show could fall apart!

'We need to have a crisis meeting,' whispered Cressida to Sophie.

That was not going to be easy. Both girls were in full costume as Yellow Feathers and Flapper. With magnificent wings and feathery make-up Lou had completed their amazing transformation from girls to birds. There was no escape without the audience seeing them - and the space backstage was very small. There was no chance of having a private discussion without the rest of the DDC overhearing.

Sophie and Cressida were trapped!

Just then John popped his head backstage.

'All ready?' he asked. It was John's job to switch off the house lights signalling the start of the show.

After that there was no going back!

Sophie and Cressida looked at each other.

'We can't start without the Trees of the Wood!' whispered Sophie in horror.

'We can't *not* start if they don't *ever* turn up,' whispered back Cress. 'Either we'd have to say the show is cancelled ... or just go ahead anyway - unless ... John could you ask Grandpa Albert if he could whizz down in Miranda to Battleaxe Barracks and see if the Trees of the Wood are still there? But remember it's top secret. If Miss Gristlegrundelblug finds out they'll be locked in and they'll never be able to perform.'

'But hurry John! Hurry! And tell Grandpa Albert to hurry!'

For the next ten agonizing minutes Sophie and Cressida waited backstage for news. Uncle Albert had set off at top speed in Miranda. He had raced down to Battleaxe Barracks. He had dived into the rhododendron bush. He had pulled the string to ring the bell. Nothing. No response from Sir Hugh whatsoever. He rang the bell again. Only one light was on in the whole building and that was downstairs in the main bay window of the front room, the best room in the house, so he guessed Miss Gristlegrundelblug would have bagged that room for herself. It seemed she was in but nobody else. He rang the bell again, pulling as hard as he dared. The bell rang far, far away. Instead of the response from Sir Hugh to his horror he saw the hall lights go on. Then the stair lights. Then the landing lights. Then one after another, at top speed, the lights popped on in each of the bedrooms upstairs as if someone was dashing from one room to the next. Then he heard a scream! It must be Miss Gristlegrundelblug! But there was still no sign of Sir Hugh and his friends.

Poor Grandpa Albert did not know what to think.

It seemed the Trees of the Wood were not at Battleaxe Barracks.

And they were not at The Barn Theatre.

Where could they be?

Perhaps they were on their way?

Grandpa Albert leapt into Miranda and speeded off back to The Barn Theatre as fast as he could to tell Sophie and Cressida the news and as slow as he could so he could keep a sharp eye out for the Trees of the Wood.

He did not notice that further up the road five trees

149

had heard the roar of Miranda's engine.

On the command ...

'Vehicle approaching - *HIDE!*'

                 ... the five trees had jumped into a little copse of fir trees.

He did not notice that the little copse of fir trees now looked five trees thicker than normal and that five of the trees were waving their arms in the wind despite there being no wind.

Neither did he hear one of the trees saying as he drove past them, 'Look it's Miranda!'

Nor did he notice the five trees rush out of the copse waving their branches even more vigorously shouting, 'Come back! Come back!'

But Grandpa Albert was racing to The Barn Theatre. There was an audience waiting and he needed to get back as quickly as possible to let Sophie and Cressida know that the Trees of the Wood had vanished!

John poked his head backstage again.

'Grandpa Albert's back. The Trees of the Wood are nowhere to be seen!'

Sophie and Cressida looked at each other stunned. *What could they do?*

It was a crisis of the most cataclysmally

catastrophic kind. The reputation of the Daisy Drama Club was on the brink!

'We'll just have to pretend they *are* here ...

'Mime it ...'

'Say the words from backstage?'

'The audience will never know ...'

The suggestions were horribly feebly feeble.

'I'll shout out the Trees of the Wood words from the lighting gallery,' suggested John helpfully. 'I don't know the words but I can read the script from up there and you can just pretend they are on stage. I'll get Grandpa Albert and Uncle Max to help me too!'

Sophie stared at John. Sometimes he could be unreliable and not concentrate and be distracted by beetles and spend more time looking at spiders than concentrating on the lighting and sometimes he could be the best brother in the world. Sophie would have hugged him but her magnificent wings and the tiny space made this impossible so she just gave him a little peck with her beak and said, 'John that is a krrracker of a brilliant idea!'

John grinned.

'Shall I turn off the house lights then?'

Sophie and Cress looked at each other. The show was about to begin and suddenly they felt terrifically, overwhelmingly excited. This moment was what all the hard work of running the Daisy Drama Club was all about and now they were determined to enjoy it - whatever happened!

'Yes! Turn off the house lights John,' said Sophie and Cress together, knowing exactly what each other was thinking as only best friends do.

'The show must go on!'

Lost and Found!

The lights dimmed and the beginners were in place. Abby had spent alot of time thinking what it would be like to be Shimmermist. She came to the conclusion she had no idea. It was only when she saw Pickle drinking from a pond and noticed the way the ripples rippled out that she got an idea. She decided to move like the ripples. This was a peculiar idea but it was the only one she had and it seemed to work and she had practised and practised her rippling movement so when it was her moment in the spotlight, she would not let the DDC down. And she did not! Shimmermist emerged mysteriously from backstage moving in a rippling, floaty, shimmeringly sort of way and said in a rippling sort of voice ...

```
Once upon a time,
On the edge of a great forest
There lived a girl and her mother ...
```

Red Riding Hood had begun!

Mrs Theodora Whistle-White had stopped feeling sick with nerves and instead brimmed with pride as Susie dazzled in the spotlight, playing the LEADING LADY to perfection. Mrs Whistle-White even managed to 'Cheep' especially cheepily when the audience shouted out the woodland creature sounds.

It was only when Lollipop suddenly started barking in Act 1 Scene 2 that she looked nervous. Mrs Theodora Whistle-White pulled her hairy coat tightly round her, thinking that at any second that ghastly sheepdog was about to attack her. Tim Stack, thinking the same, tightened his grip on Lollipop's lead. But Lollipop was not growling at the big, hairy beast. She was growling at something scratching at the barn door.

The next moment the door slowly opened and a branch waved its way in.

Susie, was on stage with Flapper and Yellow

Feathers, supposedly in the wood. Susie was dismayed to find there were no Trees of the Wood for her to wonder in and out of, carrying her basket of goodies and Granny Cold Survival Kit, but being a true professional she carried on regardless.

```
ROSE Here is the wood
     Full of WOODLAND CREATURES
```

Hearing their woodland creatures sound cue again the audience went wild ...

It was the perfect moment for Sir Hugh, who was outside the barn with his little band of trees to call out, '*OPERATION TREEFALL : Section B : part (vi)*!'

With that the Trees of the Wood burst in through the barn doors and charged onto the stage!

The audience thought this was all part of the performance; Sophie and Cressida breathed a sigh of relief. Uncle Max and Grandpa Albert, up in the lighting gallery with John, were so looking forward to being Trees of the Wood that they joined in anyway:

```
We are the Trees of the Wood,
Some are bad and some are good!
We are the Trees of the Wood,
Some are bad and some are good!

(WISPY VOICE) I'm very beautiful.
(SIR HUGH) I'm very strong.
(MISS WINDRUSH) I'm very l ... l ... long!
(JIM THE HAT) I'm very bendy.
(NO VOICE) I can sing a song ... La!

We are the Trees of the Wood
Some are bad ...
```

Suddenly there was a crash and the barn door flew open again. In burst a dramatic figure, wrapped in a black cloak and hood!

'They've gone!' it cried. 'Disappeared! Has anyone seen them? My five creaky old people?'

On stage the trees seemed paralysed in fear ...

Then one, the smallest of all, whispered in horror, 'Miss Gristlegrundelblug! Aaaaaaah!'

'Shh! She might not recognise us,' hissed Sir Hugh. 'Just keep waving your arms about like real trees!'

Miss Gristlegrundelblug - the wicked matron with the horrible hairy legs as thick as tree trunks, the murky glasses with glass so murky you can't see where she is looking, the massive curly hair where she keeps a pet lizard, the voice so deep that it rumbles like a volcano, the ears so enormous she can hear your most secret thoughts - threw back her hood to reveal a beautiful woman with lovely long blond curly hair, blue eyes and pink cherry lips.

'Has anyone seen them?' she cried again, in a voice as soft and sweet as honey, her eyes swimming with tears. 'My adorable creaky old people who I care for have disappeared! And they are all so poorly with terrible coughs and colds and splutterings that something dreadful might happen to them if they have wondered out into the cold night air!'

'Did you say five creaky old people?' shouted Grandpa Albert, as loud as a foghorn, from up in the lighting gallery.

The audience swivelled their heads to see Grandpa Albert leaning over the lighting gallery rail. They were now finding the plot a little hard to follow but it was certainly exciting!

'Oh I did! I did!'

'There they are,' said Grandpa Albert. 'On the stage ... right now!'

And, with no idea that he was talking to the infamous Miss Gristlegrundelblug, he pointed a bony old hand at the Trees of the Wood.

The lady in the cloak gave a shriek as sweet as syrup on a warm pancake and leapt with the grace of a gazelle onto the stage.

The Trees of the Wood shuffled in panic.

'Oh it *is* you!' she cried ecstatically. 'How silly of me not to recognise you straight away! Oh my dear Sir Hugh,' she cried, embracing each tree in turn. 'Oh adorable Jim! My darling Miss Windrush! Dearest wispy voice! Adorable voice that never speaks! Thank goodness you are all safe and well! All recovered from your nasty sniffs and snuffles. Because you were all so poorly I dashed out earlier to get a big box of medicine but when I returned you had all vanished! I have been nearly ill myself with worry! But here you are, right as rain! You were right,' she said turning to look up at Grandpa Albert, 'they are all here and all perfectly well!'

Miss Gristlegrundelblug smiled up at the lighting gallery with a smile as bright as the summer sunshine and as she smiled she got little dimples in her cheeks.

'Good heavens!' cried Uncle Max who was standing by Grandpa Albert. 'John, swivel the spotlight onto Miss Gristlegrundel-whatsit. Yes! I'm right! I'd recognise those dimples anywhere. There you are at last! My lovely-missing-wife-to-be! I've been looking for you for years and years and years and years! But how strange you did not see the 'LOST! Woodcutter's lovely-missing-wife-to-be' poster in the village with a portrait of you with a likeness so perfectly captured by Alice ...'

Alice beamed with pleasure.

'I did see a wonderful 'LOST! Woodcutter's lovely-missing-wife-to-be' poster,' said Miss Gristle-grundelblug sweetly, 'and was most surprised that *another* poor lovely-missing-wife-to-be had suffered exactly the same misfortune as me. But *that* lovely-missing-wife-to-be had a large moustache and big bushy eyebrows and I knew a lovely-missing-wife-to-be that hairy could not be me so I didn't ...'

One of the trees coughed in embarrassment.

'My fault!' it snapped sharply. 'Just thought if you were found we would lose you! So gave you a hairy disguise. Sorry, a bit selfish ...'

'Well really!' burst out Alice. The snappy sharp lady had drawn all over her beautiful poster!

'The poster always was a bit of a long shot,' sighed Max.

But Miss Gristlegrundelblug's smile was becoming more and more radiant as she looked up at Uncle Max.

'Max. Is it really you, Max?' she cried. 'You *sound* like my long lost Max the Woodcutter but that beard ...the Max *I* knew wasn't *that* beardy.'

'Oh I can explain *my* hairiness,' said Uncle Max. 'When you were my lovely-wife-to-be I got trapped under a tree for seven whole days and my beard grew and grew and there was nothing I could do to stop it getting bushier and bushier. When I eventually escaped and got to the church where you had been waiting so patiently you had just left to wander the world looking for me. I know that because you left me this note!'

Uncle Max held up the note that his lovely-wife-to-be had left at the church.

'Oh Max the Woodcutter. It *is* you!' cried Miss Gristlegrundelblug. 'To think I have found both my lovely-husband-to-be and my creaky old people on the same night. Oh! I am the luckiest woman alive!'

And with that Miss Gristlegrundelblug fainted.

Uncle Max leapt over the lighting balcony, bounded onto the stage and picked up Miss Gristlegrundelblug in his strong arms as if she weighed no more than a piece of confetti. He patted her pretty cheeks.

'Wake up Millie! Wake up Millie!'

'Wake up Miss Gristlegrundelblug!' yelled Grandpa Albert from the balcony.

The audience, thinking it was all part of the play joined in.

'WAKE UP MISS GRISTLEGRUNDELBLUG!'

Millie woke up.

'Why is it everyone calls me Miss Gristlegrundelblug?' she asked gazing lovingly at Uncle Max.

Sir Hugh cleared his voice.

'This is where we, the creaky old people come in. We thought it would make our dull and dreary lives more exciting if we had a wicked, mean matron with a mean name like Miss Gristlegrundelblug who had hairy legs as thick as tree trunks, who we had to escape from.'

'Then *you* came along,' snapped Miss Windrush, 'and you were far too nice. And 'Millie' is far too nice and sweet a name.'

'So we had to pretend,' said Jim the Hat.

'We had to pretend you had legs as thick as tree trunks and ...'

'That's why we couldn't just walk out of the house saying we were in a play. We had to *escape* which made it much more fun!' added the wispy lady.

'When really you are so kind to us all the time, bringing us cups of steaming tea, hot water bottles, baking cakes, ironing our underwear, knitting us cosy jumpers, plumping up our pillows, mending our clothes, putting bluebells in our bedrooms, squeezing fresh orange juice, making sure we always have a merry fire burning in the grate, baking birthday cakes ...'

'Oh, you are funny!' said Millie giggling. 'I'm just glad I found you quickly and that after all these years I have found Max the Woodcutter too!'

Uncle Max smiled sheepishly.

'Millie,' he said. 'Could I ask you something?'

'Of course, dear Max! You can ask me *anything*.'

'Would you like to come and watch the rest of the play from the lighting gallery?'

'That would be delightful!' replied Millie, smiling her dimply smile.

As Uncle Max and Millie left the stage, the audience stood up to applaud as the re-united couple walked arm in arm up to the lighting gallery.

All this time Sophie and Cressida had been on stage flapping their wings and watching the astonishing events unfurl before them. But what they both also realised and what they both knew the other was thinking as only best friends do is that the show must go on! And so they improvised ...

```
FLAPPER and YELLOW FEATHERS
   And so the Trees of the Wood
   Promised never to call Millie
   'Miss Gristlegrundelblug' ever again.
```

And the Trees of the Wood improvised back ...

Never again!

Even Abby managed to help pull it all together:

But would Rose be saved
By Will the Woodcutter?
Let's find out!

Improvisation over, Beaky as prompt was relieved that the play seemed to be following the script again. Wolfee ran ahead and locked Grandmama in the cupboard, Rose found Grandmama in bed ... at least she *thought* it was Grandmama ...

Wolfee locks Grandmama in the cupboard.
Wolfee gets into Grandmama's bed.
Wolfee is wearing Grandmama's specs and bed cap.
Rose knocks on the door of Grandmama's cottage.

WOLFEE Come in my dear,
   You have nothing to fear!

ROSE Oh goodness Grandmama,
   What big ears you've got!

WOLFEE All the better to hear you with,
   My dear.

ROSE Oh goodness, Grandmama,
   What big eyes you've got!

```
WOLFEE All the better to see you with,
   My dear.
ROSE Oh goodness, Grandmama,
   What big teeth you've got!

WOLFEE All the better to
   ... eat you with!

ROSE Help!
   This beast thinks I'm a feast!
   Help! Help! Help!
```

Will the Woodcutter dashed in and the fight between Wolfee and Will was a swashbuckling sensation - Sir Hugh could barely contain his excitement.

'Whack him! Block! Block! Block! Lunge! Through the audience! Swing from the lighting gallery! Backstage! Defend! Block! Block! Over Mrs Whistle-White's head! Block! Block!'

The battle came to a triumphant finale which not only ended the fight but finished Miss Gristlegrundelblug for good. Will the Woodcutter grabbed the painting of Miss Gristlegrundelblug off the wall and smashed it down over the head of Wolfee. The audience gasped. Wolfee crashed to the floor, dead as a doormat and Miss Gristlegrundelblug got the smash-bang-wallop end she deserved!

At the final bow Susie and the cast were bombarded by bunches and bunches of flowers that Mrs Theodora Whistle-White had brought along to throw on stage. Susie blushed but she didn't mind. It wasn't so bad being in the spotlight after all! Only when Mrs Theodora Whistle-White started shouting 'Splendid! Sensational! A triumph!' did Susie have a twinge of embarrassment.

But a triumph it was thought Sophie and Cressida. A triumph over the many twists and turns and near disasters. Now they just enjoyed the best feeling in the world - another successful performance for the Daisy Drama Club!

Double Dimples

The day after the show the Daisy Drama Club were back in The Barn Theatre tidying up when a horn hooted and into the drive drove Uncle Max with Millie in his old banger, and an old boot and a *JUST MARRIED* sign tied to the bumper.

'I've bought you a basket of goodies,' said Millie hopping out, 'to say thank you. If you had not put on your play I might *never* have found Max again. Even though we were living so close I would never have recognised him with that big bushy beard.'

Sophie stared at Uncle Max. He had trimmed his beard right back and for the first time in her whole life she could sort of see what he looked like.

'You look tho handthome, Uncle Max!' said Susie. 'Are you Mrs Max now Millie?'

'Yes,' said Millie. 'The Right Rev Marbles married us this morning. We were worried one of us might get lost again so we decided to carry on from where we left off all those years ago, which was at the altar.'

'How romantic!' said Susie clapping her hands in delight. 'Where will you live?'

'I could never leave my creaky old people at Bluebell House so dear Max is going to come and live there too!'

'Bluebell House? I thought it was called Battleaxe Barracks?'

'Oh that's just the funny name my creaky old people have given it! It's real name is Bluebell House and it's quite the loveliest place to live in the world!'

Millie beamed, showing her dimples.

Uncle Max beamed and for the first time ever, Sophie could see he too had dimples!

Later that afternoon Sophie and Cressida sat out in the garden considering events.

'We chose *Red Riding Hood* because it would be simple and easy to do,' said Sophie.

'Mmm but lots of things happened that we could never have expected to happen,' added Cressida picking some daisies and threading them together to make a daisy chain. 'It's strange how one thing always leads to another.'

The sky was blue and the sun warm.

Summer was on its way.

That left just one thing to think about ...

... the next production
for the Daisy Drama Club!

Did you know ...

... you really CAN put on

the Daisy Drama Club's

Red Riding Hood!

Just email

scripts@beetleheart.co.uk

and we'll send you all the info!

Love from the

daisy drama club

daisy drama club
STAGE FRIGHT!
belinda roberts

daisy drama club
ON TOUR!
belinda roberts

by belinda roberts

BOOKS

daisy drama club

- Stage Fright! - Daisy Drama Club
- Spotlight! - Daisy Drama Club
- On Tour - Daisy Drama Club

- Mr Darcy Goes Overboard
(Sourcebooks)

PLAYS

- Angelica ... and the Monstrous, Monster of the Deep *
(Samuel French)
- Scrooge! *
- Beetleheart *
- Rose! ... and the Wicked Wolfee *
- Christmas Candy *
- Daydream Believer *
- OTMA's Glory
- Vivaldi's Angels
- Starry Night
- Pride, Pop and Prejudice
- The Frog Princess
- Trio : Creation • Jonah • The Real Mother

(* performed by the original Daisy Drama Club)

www.beetleheart.co.uk